# IN HIS COLLAR

PATRICIA D. EDDY

Editing by Clare C. Marshall

Cover Design by Fiona Jayde Media

## JUST FOR YOU

Join my Unstoppable Readers' Group for sneak peeks, behind the scenes updates from my writing cave, and more. http://patriciadeddy.com.

**A favor...**

After you finish this book, you'd make my day if you'd take a few moments to leave a review and tell your friends about *In His Collar*. You can leave a review where you purchased the book and on Goodreads.

# 1

**Nick**

"I NEED TO ASK YOU SOMETHING." Lia's hand trembled as she touched Nick's arm. She kept her gaze downcast, focusing on his glass of scotch.

"Anything, love." Nick toyed with a lock of her hair as he glanced up from the financial reports his admin had thrust upon him moments before he'd left work that evening. Faint smudges bruised her eyes and Nick searched her face. "You look knackered. Is your roommate still playing his drums at all hours of the night? You know you could simply move in with me, yeah?"

Blond curls tumbled over her shoulders as she pulled her hair clip loose and shook her head. "I'm not ready to give up my apartment. Neither are you."

"We've been together for three years. You've worn my collar for two." He drew his finger along the platinum choker. A diamond in the shape of a heart dangled from the chain. The day she'd agreed to the collaring, he'd thought his life complete. "We'll make things work. Move in."

Lia's blue eyes clouded. "And then what? If you want me to share your home, you have to be willing to talk about our future, about sharing a life with me. And every time I bring up the subject, you—"

"We're happy, yeah? Why can't that be enough?"

Her lower lip wobbled for a breath, and then she sighed. "I suppose it has to be." She toyed with the diamond, her cheeks pale. When she met his gaze, fear swam in her eyes. "I have a doctor's appointment tomorrow. They want to run some tests. Just routine. I...haven't been sleeping well lately. I need you to unlock the collar. No metal in the MRI machine."

"Of course." Nick set his scotch on the side table, reached around Lia, and undid the clasp. In truth, it didn't lock, but the multiple catches required two hands and had to be released in a particular order. As the collar tumbled free, Nick cupped Lia's cheek. "Is this serious? Do you want me to go with you?"

"No." With one hard blink, her face transformed, the worry fading away. "Just a precaution. Probably a vitamin deficiency or I'm working too hard. My doctor's just being thorough."

Nick nodded. "You do spend too much time at the office. The Jimmy Fund has run you ragged the past few months. I'm so proud of the work you do, Lia, but you need a vacation."

"Like you can talk about that." Lia jabbed him in the shoulder, knocking the financial reports into his lap. "Mr. I'm Going To Buy Another Small Country Before Bedtime."

"Only a tanker, my darling. The country will wait until next week." Nick tossed the bound report onto the floor, then scooped Lia into his arms. "Should we celebrate this particular tanker?"

"Why not?"

She laughed as he carried her upstairs to his bedroom. So light. Had she lost weight recently? No, his new personal trainer had been particularly hard on him the past few months. Lia was perfect, and as he stripped off her sweatshirt, her breasts beckoned him.

"I love your body, Lia. My gorgeous sub. So perfect." Nick sucked one pert nipple into his mouth, and she moaned under his ministrations, pressing her body to his and draping her arms around his neck. "Now," he said as he kissed his way over to the other breast. "Shall I bind you?"

"Yes, Sir. Please."

**Six months later**

The infernal beeping wouldn't shut up. Nick shook himself awake, the pain in his back and neck sending sparks racing all the way down his legs. Where was he? Shite. As Lia struggled to breathe in the sterile hospital bed, Nick dropped his head into his hands.

The cancer had left her a shell of her former self. Barely eighty pounds, she hadn't been out of bed in more than a week, and though she'd begged him to take her to his home, to let her die somewhere other than the hospital, the doctors were adamant about keeping her here. He'd listened, and now...she'd be lucky to make it another day.

He'd been a bloody idiot.

*Fuck it.*

Texting his driver, Nick hoped he wasn't too late.

When the man promised to arrive in less than ten minutes, Nick blew out a breath.

Perhaps she'd have enough time.

"Lia, darling?" Nick brushed his knuckles across her cheek. "Wake up for me."

"Nick," she croaked, her chapped lips barely moving. As she

forced her lids open, he saw the truth in her gaze. Not a day. Hours at best.

"We're going home, love. Can you hold on a little longer for me?"

The fire in her bloodshot eyes staggered him. Even as weak as she was, she'd fight for this. "Hurry."

Nick ignored the nurses when they tried to stop him from carrying Lia down the hall to the elevator. Wrapped in a blanket, she shuddered in his arms, each breath rattling in her chest like a bag of pennies. Her DNR mandated no heroic measures, or he'd have insisted on a breathing tube.

How could he have let her go? When she'd refused to put the collar back on after the medical tests, she'd said she needed space. He hadn't listened to the words she didn't say. The way she'd kept her gaze on her clasped hands, the pallor of her skin. He'd given her that space—too angry and selfish to see what was right in front of him.

Now, her cool limbs so thin he feared he'd crush her, he thanked God for these last few minutes with her. Once inside the limo, he ordered his driver to break every traffic law necessary to reach his home in under fifteen minutes.

The man deserved a raise. Twelve minutes later, Nick climbed into bed with Lia. "We're home, love."

"Thank you," she whispered. "Don't...leave."

The house could have collapsed around them, and he wouldn't have let go of her. "I don't want to live without you," he managed through the sob that tried to burst from his throat. Tears gathered in his eyes. "I should have given you everything you ever wanted, but—"

"Shh." Her fingers fluttered weakly on his. "You...gave...me this. I...love...you."

A single tear slipped from the corner of her eye, and she buried her face in his neck. He gathered her against him, her stuttering breath hot against his skin. "I love you, Lia."

He repeated the words over and over again until her entire body went slack, and she breathed her list. Only then, did Nick let himself cry.

# 2

Eight years later

## Nick

*I SHOULDN'T BE HERE.*

Nick ran a hand through his dark blond hair, tugging on an unruly tuft behind his ear. Flashing his ID at the bouncer—as if he looked under twenty-one and wasn't one of the most recognizable men in Boston—he followed Terrance through the doors of Bound.

The heavy, slow beat of the music set his nerves on edge. He'd planned a different sort of night. A bottle of eighteen-year-old Macallan, greasy pizza, and bitter regrets. Instead, he'd left the bottle unopened on his counter, the pizza order unsent, and his regrets casting a shadow over his soul.

*Eight years.*

Grief faded in the face of the all-too-familiar itch skittering over his skin. *No.* He dipped his hand into his pocket and fingered his eighteen-month chip. Stupid, thinking that a piece of metal could stop the desire to call his bookie, but the smooth pattern under his fingertips calmed the urge enough for him to breathe again.

"Drink?" Terrance gestured to the bar.

"Yeah." Despite the no-alcohol policy the BDSM club maintained during the week, the bar took up half the wall and lights reflected off dozens of colorful bottles. Nick dropped onto a stool and scanned the shelves, hoping for a menu—or at least some indication of what the hell he was looking at while Terrance wandered over to the railing in the corner of the room.

"What'll it be?" The bartender, her black curls tumbling over her right eye in an angular bob, flashed him a smile. "Let me guess. You're new here?"

"That obvious?" Nick nodded towards the bottles. "What're my options? Juice and sparkling water?"

The woman, whose skin sparkled slightly under the lights, pinned him with a hard stare, and a tiny furrow between her brows begged to be smoothed away. "If you trust me, I have something a little more interesting for you."

"Why not?" He probably wouldn't finish the drink anyway. Though he prided himself on clean eating and only a modicum of alcohol, he ached to get plastered tonight, and that wouldn't happen here.

Terrance pulled out the stool next to Nick. "Sorry. The shibari exhibition on the main stage distracted me. They're having another show in twenty minutes."

Years ago, the ancient art of Japanese rope tying would have stirred Nick's dominant desires. Tonight, he managed only a single nod in acknowledgment.

"Supposed to be fantastic," the bartender offered with a breathy edge to her voice. She tipped one of the bottles, sending a shot of caramel-colored liquid cascading into the cocktail shaker. "The owner brought in some experts from New York City. One night only." After slamming a glass down on top of the shaker, she nodded at Terrance. "Can I get you something, hon?"

"Bottle of water." The doctor pulled a twenty from his wallet and nodded at Nick. "This cover both of us?"

"Yep. Five bucks in change, too."

"Keep it," Terrance said, snagging the bottle she'd set in front of him and turning to Nick. "I'm going to wander a bit. Meet me down by the stage in fifteen?"

Nick glanced at his watch. "Fine."

As the petite brunette poured Nick's drink into a rocks glass, he turned and scanned the top floor of the club. Women gathered at the railing, peering down at the stage one floor below. The blonde directly across from him wore a thin, white collar around her neck. A relative newbie looking to play with a willing Dom or Master. At the other end of the railing, a woman in a bright red corset and spiked heels fingered a black collar with four metal rings attached.

Her Master approached, and she dropped her gaze to the floor. The man held out his hand, and the sub allowed him to lead her away.

"Earth to...um...Sir? Let me know what you think." The bartender nudged the drink closer. Nick shook his head to clear the memories that threatened him and turned back to the pretty brunette.

"Not Sir. Nick." He didn't want any part of the lifestyle at the moment. Why had he let Terrance talk him into coming out tonight? Rubbing a hand over his chin, Nick met the bartender's gaze.

"You're wearing a Dom's mark." She gestured to the stamp on the back of his hand. "Plus, you just have that look. And as your friend paid in cash, I couldn't cheat and snag your name from your credit card."

*Shite.* Of course. The last club Nick had frequented mandated the use of bracelets and collars for subs and armbands for Doms and Masters. Bound had no such rules, but stamped everyone's hand with either a *D* or an *s* upon entry.

The deep burgundy drink in front of him looked like cherry soda, but when he took a sip, the smoky taste of aged scotch mixed with a hint of currant and sage surprised him. "You're not breaking the rules, are you...?" Nick cocked a brow.

"Sofia." She grinned, and the light in her smile reached all the way to her brown eyes. "No cheating. Experimenting. That's a smoked shrub muddled with half a sugar cube and a couple of secret ingredients. None of which are alcoholic."

"Your recipe?" Nick took another sip and found he didn't miss the buzz of alcohol at all. Sofia was every bit as intoxicating, from her proud smile to the way her triumphant gaze held his.

Her head bobbed as she swiped a towel over the bar. "You're my first victim. I've been begging the bar manager to let me play around with some custom recipes for months. Don't tell anyone, though. He never gave me the official okay. But he's not here tonight, and I feel like living dangerously. Plus, you looked like you needed something strong." Sofia winked at him. "I figured if you hated it, I'd finish it for you, and no one would be the wiser."

Nick laughed, and something inside his chest threatened to break free. He shouldn't be having fun on the anniversary of Lia's death, but he didn't have much in his life to laugh over these days.

"Hey, you okay?" Sofia leaned forward, resting a hand on his arm. The warmth of her fingers seeped through the expensive fabric of his shirt, and as she squeezed lightly, something stirred inside him. "I feel like we've met before."

"I'd remember you, Sofia," he replied as he slid off the stool. "I'm solid. Thank you for the drink." He downed the last of her "experiment" and set the glass on the bar. "I should go find my friend."

Her lips curved into a gentle frown for a moment until she caught herself. "See ya around, Nick."

After two interminable hours of wandering aimlessly among the crowds, and another of Sofia's mystery drinks, Nick ached to go home. The gorgeous bartender provided the only glimpse of light this evening, but if he went back again, he worried she'd mark him as a creep—or as Nicholas Fairhaven, which might be worse.

The shibari demonstration left a sour taste in Nick's mouth. The Dom didn't check on his sub often enough, and the woman's right arm had gone numb by the time the demonstration was over. None of the club's Masters walking the floor had noticed the sub's fingers turning a darker shade of pink than the rest of her skin, but Nick had. He'd flagged down an employee and suggested ending the demonstration early, but the guy grunted something that sounded like "fuck off" before stalking away.

Now, a headache brewed behind his eyes, and he longed to go home. His text message to Terrance still unanswered, he wandered down a long hallway behind the bar, hoping to find his friend and beg off for the night.

He peeked into a couple of the semi-private rooms. In one, a Domme had her sub on all fours and was whipping his arse with a leather crop. Next door, a woman strapped to a St. Andrew's Cross whimpered as her Master trailed an ice cube over her skin. A third room marked *Private* had a numeric lock on the door, but Nick paused, positive he heard a man's triumphant cry behind it. The heavy bass of the club's music changed, masking any other sounds from within, and he shrugged and continued down the hall.

Rounding a corner, he heard Terrance's voice cut through the din.

"What's your safeword, my dear?"

"Red, sir." A statuesque redhead in a skin-tight dress that looked to be nothing more than a handful of artfully arranged straps reclined on a glossy black table, her arms bound over her head. Terrance dragged a suede flogger over the woman's bare thigh, and she shuddered.

Meeting Nick's gaze, Terrance smiled and waved him into the room. "Melody dear, I came here with a friend. Do you mind if he watches us?"

"No, Sir. I'd...like that." The way she batted her eyes as she answered had Nick shaking his head. He and Terrance had played together before, taking turns with a delightful sub a few years prior. But Nick had adopted a rather monkish lifestyle since his last live-in slave, Candy. As he watched Terrance take control, gently commanding Melody, Nick's heart ached, and the emptiness in his soul drowned him. Despite the lack of stimulating conversation, Candy had eased his loneliness for a time. Until suddenly, she hadn't, and he'd turned to horses and blackjack to fill the void. He didn't want to play anymore. Didn't want the casual scenes the clubs offered. He wanted a partner.

After Nick mouthed "have fun," he slipped out of the room.

A lull in the music provided him a moment's peace until a woman's scream carried into the hall.

*What the fuck?*

The woman screamed again, and the tenor changed to one of pure, unadulterated terror. Nick took off at a run, and three doors down another dark hallway, he skidded to a halt. A burly man clad in a dark blue suit had a woman pressed against the wall in the corner of one of the private rooms, her wrists pinned in one meaty palm.

"Shut the fuck up," the man growled as he covered the girl with his bulky frame. "I'm not supposed to damage you, but that can be arranged."

"Hey!" Nick called from the doorway. "What the fuck do you think you're doing?"

The woman met his gaze, fear widening her eyes. "Help me," she whimpered.

The Dom—not that he deserved that title—glared at Nick. "If you don't want to end up in a world of hurt, you'll walk out that door," the man spat. "Now."

"I don't think so, mate. The lady doesn't want whatever you're offering." Though the man had at least six inches and a hundred pounds on Nick, he couldn't walk away. Nick sighted a panic button next to the light switch. Striding into the room, he'd almost reached the red knob when the brute whirled, driving a fist into Nick's stomach and sending him sprawling back into the hall.

The woman, now crumpled on the floor, tried to get up, but the Dom pounced on her, pulling something from his pocket. Metal glinted in the spotlights. Fighting for breath, Nick got to his feet and blinked, hard.

A syringe.

Nick sprang for the man's arm but took an elbow to the chin instead. The impact darkened his vision, and he stumbled back. Only dimly aware of the woman's whimper, Nick gritted his teeth and tried to clear his head. The syringe clattered to the floor, and the thug pulled his limp victim into his arms.

Only six feet from the panic button now, Nick sprinted forward and slapped his hand over the red knob, then set his shoulders and rammed into the would-be-kidnapper's gut. The unconscious woman slumped to the floor as the two men grappled. "No fucking way you're taking her anywhere," Nick grunted as he landed a punch to the guy's cheek.

Two of the club's Masters darkened the door, and the attacker pulled a gun. Nick grabbed his arm, trying to wrestle the pistol from the man's grip. "Gun!"

The Masters ducked seconds before Nick's ears screamed in protest. Disoriented, he staggered back as splinters fell from the ceiling. The gunman went for the girl again, but Nick had already reached her side. "You'll have to shoot me," he growled.

For a split second, he thought the guy might actually do it, but muffled shouts echoed from the hall. The attacker pointed the gun at the guards. "Back up. Now."

Once the doorway was clear, the woman's would-be-kidnapper slipped out the door. Shouts echoed from down the hall, along with a scream. But then a door slammed.

Nick pulled the unconscious woman into his arms, brushing brown curls away from her face. Bruises darkened her neck, her wrists, and her upper arms. "You're all right," he murmured, though he doubted she could hear him.

"Is that—?"

"Nicholas Fairhaven?"

Voices from the hall competed with the ringing in his ears, and Nick looked up to see a handful of patrons snapping pictures of him holding a beaten, unconscious woman with a syringe on the floor in front of him.

*Shit.*

## 3

Nick

THE EMTS WHEELED the sobbing girl on the gurney down the hall. Nick held an ice pack to his jaw as across from him, a detective scribbled in his notebook. Stuck in the club owner's tiny office that smelled vaguely of sweat and sex, he'd answered every question at least twice already, and his patience had fled half an hour ago.

"When did you see the syringe?" Detective Sampson asked.

"For the third time," Nick said, "I heard the girl scream. When I entered the room, I thought the arse was an untrained Dom until he pulled the syringe out of his pocket. Why don't you simply check the security cameras?" He glanced over at Victor, the club's owner, leaning against the desk. "Since you seem to have some question as to my part in this whole mess, you should be able to catch the two of them entering the room."

Victor held Nick's stare. "The security cameras are broken. There is no footage."

After rolling his eyes, Nick returned his focus to the detective. "Do you honestly think that with a face as well-known as mine,

I'd try a stunt like that in a public venue? Or at all? For fuck's sake, I'm not that dumb."

The detective sighed and shook his head. "No, Mr. Fairhaven. I suppose not. But the pictures showing up on social media are pretty scandalous. My sergeant would have my badge if I didn't push. I need to interview a few other witnesses. Would you mind waiting in the front room for half an hour or so? I may have more questions before I'm done."

"You couldn't simply ring me in the morning? It's after midnight." Nick fought to maintain a civil tone. He had a pretty good idea what the photos showed—and how his brother would react to them. Ben would have to do some damage control. At least the girl—if she remembered anything—would confirm his story.

"I'd rather not, sir."

Trying not to groan, Nick shook his head. "Fine. I'll wait around." He trudged out of the office, tossing the ice pack in a trash can in the hall. What a difference a few lights made. Once the police had arrived, the owner had shut the place down and turned on the overheads, and the dark, seductive space had transformed into a cold, harsh, industrial warehouse.

Out in the main room, a handful of employees lingered, including the two staff Masters who'd chased the suspect. Nick's gaze slid to the bar, where Sofia stifled a yawn as she hunched over a thick book.

*Stop staring*, he chided himself, but under the bright lights, the skin under her eyes swelled and darkened, and she twisted a lock of her hair around a delicate finger. She wasn't his type. He'd always gravitated towards trim, tall blondes, but something about the petite and curvy raven-haired bartender rooted him to the floor, unable to look away.

As if she sensed his scrutiny, she looked up, then smiled. "Nick, right? Are you okay?"

Tugged closer by an invisible thread, he offered her a weary grin. "Well enough. What are you still doing here? And what smells so good?"

"Can't leave the bar untended until I lock up the cash register. The owner isn't responding to my text messages." Her slim shoulders curved inward as she sighed. "Everyone left is pretty shaken up, so I tried another experiment." She gestured towards a glass carafe filled with a steaming concoction that resembled strong tea. "Want some?"

He wanted a real drink—and the comforts of home—but Sofia's voice carried a note of sadness, and curiosity got the better of him. Taking a seat, he asked, "What's in this one?"

"Ginger, honey, more of the smoked shrub, and chamomile." She poured a generous mug for him and one for herself.

"How does one smoke a shrub?" Nick took a sip, marveling at the rich flavors. "And why aren't you selling that knowledge for a very large sum of money?"

Sofia laughed as she closed the textbook: *Comprehensive Theories of Psychotherapy.* "Because very few places care about making fancy non-alcoholic drinks. Though if you mix this stuff with bourbon, it's fucking awesome."

"Too bad you don't have any." Nick's phone buzzed in his pocket, and he tried not to crack a molar as he read Alex's text message.

*Nicholas, what the fuck is going on? The Babbler's accusing you of being addicted to heroin. And implying that the woman you were with tonight overdosed. I hope you have a very good explanation for that photo. The Board is never going to allow you back after this.*

"Bloody hell," Nick muttered under his breath. When he met Sofia's gaze, concern darkened her brown eyes. "My brother is upset with me."

She slid her drink next to his, then walked gingerly around to the front of the bar, hopped onto the stool next to him, and kicked off her heels. "How come?"

"You haven't seen the photos all over the internet?" Nick tapped his phone screen and brought up the *Beantown Babbler.* *Is billionaire playboy Nicholas Fairhaven addicted to heroin? Playboy's companion ODs at local BDSM club.*

Sofia gaped. "For fuck's sake. You saved that girl. And they're going to claim you're on drugs?" Her eyes narrowed, though a hint of light danced in them. "Wait. You're not on drugs, right?"

He snorted. "Never so much as smoked a joint. I chose another vice. And I'm in recovery for that one." At her confused gaze, he shrugged. "Gambling. You didn't know?"

As she combed her fingers through her inky locks, her cheeks reddened. "I don't get out a lot. When you introduced yourself earlier, I thought you looked familiar, but I didn't know why."

"I find that hard to believe." At Sofia's arched brows, Nick kicked himself. "That you don't get out much."

She gestured at the bar. "I work here Sunday through Thursday nights. Weekends, I'm the lunch hostess at Wicked Good Cafe. The rest of the time, I'm studying. Unless you count glancing at the gossip headlines at the supermarket—they're right there at checkout, kind of hard to miss—I haven't paid much attention to anything other than political news in..." The furrow deepened between her brows and Nick forced himself to keep his hands clasped around his mug lest he smooth the tiny line away. "Well, let's just say it's been a long time."

"Sofia!" Victor shouted from the hall. "Put your fucking shoes back on and close up the bar."

"Bastard," she muttered as she hopped off the stool, thrust her feet into her stilettos with a wince, and stalked towards the owner. "You've got the keys. I already closed out and sent Stephan to the bank drop. If you'd responded to any of my text messages, maybe I wouldn't have missed my ride home."

Victor gestured to his office, and after shooting Nick an exasperated look, Sofia followed.

**Sofia**

"I need to know what that man said to you." Victor shut the door of one of the privacy rooms and gestured to a chair.

Sofia shook her head. "I wouldn't sit in one of these rooms if you doubled my salary. And he didn't say anything to me. We talked about drinks."

"You know who he is?" The big man crossed his arms over his barrel chest and glared down at her.

When she started working at Bound, that stare intimidated her, and she'd have backed down, cowering. Not anymore. In a few weeks, she wouldn't need this job anymore, and she'd be able to get the hell out from under his poor management skills and angry attitude. "I do now."

*Oh God. What if he was here for one of Victor's parties?*

Victor stalked into her personal space, backing her up against the wall. When his hand stroked her throat, Sofia locked her gaze on his. With a dozen cops milling around the club, he wouldn't hurt her. No, this was only an intimidation tactic—one she wouldn't fall for.

"If he wants in the game, you'll tell me immediately. Do you understand?" With desire etched on his face, Victor tightened his fingers. Not enough to close off her airway, but enough that her heart raced.

"Yes. I understand. Big names. Deep pockets. Don't offer any information unless they ask. You don't think I know the drill after three years?"

His hand fell away. "Good. I knew I could trust you, Sofia."

*Like hell you did.*

When Victor pressed the cash register key into her hand and

then slipped out of the privacy room, Sofia let out a shaky breath. "Two or three more weeks. Then it won't matter."

With a quick glance at the stairwell, Sofia verified that the door remained locked. Had there been a game tonight? She couldn't remember. Victor never warned her when he was hosting one of his poker games. The men rarely visited the bar. No, Victor kept his own stash of hard alcohol up there. Whenever a rich or powerful man came into the club, however, he ordered her to feel them out, see if they'd be interested in joining the game. Thankfully, Bound wasn't a big club, and she'd only had to do his dirty work once, two years ago.

But Nick Fairhaven...the billionaire with a gambling problem...had he been here to scene? Or to play poker?

As she returned to the main room, she found Nick sitting on one of the benches by the railing with his head in his hands. Shoulders slumped, his blond hair mussed, sadness surrounded him like a dark cloud. His empty mug of tea sat on the bar next to her textbook.

Without a word, she locked up the register, gathered her things, and poured them both more tea. Something about the man begged for connection, for comfort, and after Victor's vague threat, she had to at least pretend to care why Nick came in tonight.

"Hey." Sofia held a mug out for him. When Nick raised his head, his lips curved, but she couldn't call the expression a smile. "I'm surprised you're still here. Want a refill?"

"Thank you. I'm afraid I'm stuck here for a bit. The police asked me to wait in case they had more questions."

"I'm sorry." She sank onto the bench next to him. "You picked a crappy night to try this place out, you know."

He laughed, a dry, derisive sound, then leaned back against the railing. "That I did. Though it wasn't my choice. A friend dragged me here."

"The guy with the water?" Sofia tried to wiggle her toes inside her shoes but only succeeded in sending sparks of pain running up her legs. "Where'd he go?"

"With the young woman to the hospital. Terrance is a doctor. My ride as well." Nick pulled out his phone and winced at a message on the screen.

"Mr. Fairhaven?" Detective Sampson emerged from the hallway. "We're done for the night. Though I'd appreciate it if you'd remain available for the next few days if we have more questions."

"Of course." Nick rose, dipped his hand into his pocket, and came up with a business card. "My mobile number. Is there any news on the young woman? Will she be all right?"

The detective's eyes clouded over, and he shifted his gaze to the side for a brief moment. "I can't answer that."

Nick sighed and gave a small shake of his head. "Very well. Good night, Detective."

Sofia sipped the last of her tea as he trudged back to the bench. "What about you? Still waiting to lock up the bar?"

"No. That's done. But all the bars around here are letting out. I'm going wait half an hour to leave. The percentage of drunks will go way down."

Nick tapped his phone screen, then frowned. "How are you getting home?"

"I'll take the T." She twirled her fare card between her fingers.

"Can I offer you a ride?"

Though the idea of walking to the subway in her heels didn't appeal to her, she didn't get into cars with strange men. Even famous ones. "I'll be fine. I make this trip...a lot. Though not usually this late."

Worry colored Nick's tone. "You don't usually have a would-be-kidnapper in your club either. I have a car service on standby. The driver can take you home, and I'll call another car for myself."

Her brows drew together, the motion aggravating her headache. "I..."

"The T-station is almost half a mile from here. If you'd prefer, call a cab. I'll pay for it." Nick pulled out his wallet. "Let me do this?"

"Why?" As she rose and stepped close enough to catch a whiff of his scent—sandalwood and a hint of tobacco—she searched his face. "You don't know me. I sold you a couple of drinks."

"You made my night better. Gave me a bit of peace on a day I would have much rather drowned in a bottle." He seemed surprised at his admission, and his cheeks flushed red. "I mean... shite. I'm tired and babbling. I don't get out much either. I was in a piss-poor mood when Terrance dragged me here. Now...I'm not. I'd like to repay you for that."

Sofia found nothing but truth in his eyes, and she pressed her lips together for a long moment. "We can share a car. Let's get out of here."

# 4

## Nick

SOFIA SMELLED like gardenias and white ginger. In the backseat of the town car, she hugged her backpack like a shield. Since her skirt left little to the imagination, he didn't blame her. "Where should the driver take you?"

"I live in the South End. On Chandler Street," she said quietly.

"That's quite a commute." Nick nodded at her backpack. "And school?"

Sofia rolled her eyes. "All the way in Chelsea." With a quick check of her phone, she huffed out a breath. "Which is going to make getting to my 9:00 a.m. exam tomorrow morning a total bitch."

"You don't sleep much, do you?" At her chuckle, he offered her a small smile. "How long have you worked at Bound?"

"Three years."

Nick cocked his head, studying the young woman across from him. Such an air of strength to her, yet, she was quite obviously no Domme. Not with the way she'd addressed him earlier. "May I ask you a personal question?"

Sofia glanced over at him, then dropped her gaze to her hands clasped around her backpack. "I suppose."

"Your boss, Victor. He's a bit of a dolt. Why do you work for him?"

"Because the tips are better than anywhere else I've ever tended bar. And I need the money. School doesn't pay for itself." She puffed out her chest a bit and straightened. "Unlike you, I can't afford to turn down a hundred more a night than I can make at a place closer to home. Even if I do have to share the money with the bar manager who can't figure out how to make a single drink."

Discomfort had Nick shifting in his seat. Yes, he was rich. Even after the events of the previous two years, no one would accuse him of living hand-to-mouth. He still owed Alexander five hundred thousand, but his financial advisor assured him that within the next two years, he'd make that back and then some. If he managed to reclaim his seat on the board—or by some miracle, his position as CEO of Fairhaven Exports—he'd be solvent again in months. Though Alexander's text messages hadn't left him very confident about that possibility.

Returning his focus to Sofia, Nick frowned. "I'm sorry. I didn't mean to pry. I simply...didn't like how he spoke to you."

"He's harmless. Well, sort of." Sofia fiddled with her backpack strap. "You don't want to get on his bad side." She narrowed her eyes, studying him. Her voice took on a subtle edge. "Or get involved with him in any way. But I only have another few weeks there."

"Oh?" Nick ignored his buzzing phone. "You're quitting?"

"Assuming I pass this exam tomorrow?" She grinned. "Yes. I just got into Boston College—Master's program. Partial scholarship. Two more paychecks, maybe three, and I'll have enough saved up for my first year. After that, I can intern with another therapist—paid. My sister's moving to Germany in a couple of weeks, and I'll be...free."

The lightness infusing her tone rubbed off on Nick, and despite the day, the police questioning, and Alexander's text messages, he didn't want the night to end. "I don't suppose you fancy a drink, do you?"

Sofia glanced down at her backpack. "I can't. It's a ninety-minute trip to Chelsea in the morning."

Disappointment flooded him. He'd spent all of half an hour with the woman at his side, but he wanted more. "Then...maybe tomorrow after your exam? Coffee?"

"Why?" The shock that roughened her tone gave way to a shyness that he found endearing as her shoulders hunched and her fingers found the strap of her bag once more, twirling the thick woven material.

How could he explain what she'd given him? A bright spot amid what was guaranteed to be the worst day of his year? A bridge over the gaping maw in his heart? He settled on the safe answer—the one he'd already given. "The same reason I offered you a ride."

She frowned at him, pondering. "One condition."

"Anything." Hope surged through him, such an unfamiliar emotion he couldn't remember the last time he'd felt this way.

Until she replied, "Tell me why you'd planned to get drunk today."

"That's...a very long story."

The driver slowed as Sofia's street stretched out before them. "Here's fine," she called up to the man. She chewed on the inside of her cheek for a moment. The motion only served to deepen the furrow between her brows. "Then we can have a snack along with that coffee. My exam will be over at eleven tomorrow. Meet me at 70 Everett Avenue. On the corner by the school gates. If you're more than five minutes late, you'll miss me."

With a quick flash of her brilliant smile, she ducked out of the car.

"Fuck me," Nick muttered to himself before giving the driver his address. "I didn't even get her number."

In his flat, Nick sank down into his father's leather chair. Sometimes he felt the man's ghost lingering, a whiff of pipe smoke floating from the cushion. What he wouldn't give for some sage advice from the old man right now. Ice rattled in his glass as he downed half the scotch in a single swallow.

Despite the brief respite from his grief—and Sofia's scent lingering—his mind wandered as he stared into the flickering orange and blue flames of the small gas fireplace.

*"Yes, Sir. Please make me come."*

Lia's soft voice comforted him—until the ice shifted. She wasn't here. Wasn't anywhere. The cancer had decimated her curves, her beautiful blond hair, her bright smile, and her sparkling eyes. Now, he had nothing left.

"Why didn't you tell me?" he asked the empty room. "Maybe I could have..."

*Saved her?* Hardly. He'd been too young. Too selfish. Too... spoiled. Hell, when she'd started getting tired halfway through their scenes, he'd pulled away—emotionally at least. No wonder she'd broken up with him after her diagnosis. Hidden the discovery of the stage four liver cancer that ate away at her, leaving nothing but hollow eyes, sunken cheeks, and her soft voice.

A tear burned in the corner of his eye. He'd been there at the end. She'd called him seventeen days before she'd died. Confessed everything. And he'd spent every second at her bedside, holding her despite the tubes and the wires and the bony edges of her wasted body.

The rest of the scotch slid down his throat, and he headed for his wet bar to pour himself another. Deep inside, the hole left by Lia's death started to grow. A vague sense of foreboding tinged the back of his throat with a sour, metallic taste that only whiskey would wash away.

When he'd poured himself a double, he wandered over to the window and then dug out his phone.

"Nick?" Cal's raspy voice carried the thickness of sleep, but he cleared his throat, and vague shuffling echoed over the line. "Give me a minute, buddy."

Nick took another swallow of scotch, and the world shimmered around him. *Getting there.* A thorough drunken stupor would cure all of his ills. Wouldn't it?

"Okay. I'm here. Talk to me."

His sponsor's voice usually calmed the itch to go to the track or call his bookie. This evening, though, he wasn't sure anything could quell the sensation. Except more alcohol. "Tonight fucking sucked."

"Did you bet? Even come close? I can be there in half an hour. Probably less," Cal said with a harsh edge to his tone.

"No." Nick flopped back in his chair. "Terrance dragged me out tonight. To a BDSM club. Pull up the *Beantown Babbler.*"

"Hang on. Got to turn on my computer." Cal groaned, and a chair squeaked. "You avoided the clubs for years, didn't you?"

"Mostly. Terrance loves them, though. And Alex didn't bother calling tonight. It was either go with Terrance or drink myself into oblivion." Nick stared at his glass. Oblivion wasn't that far out of reach.

Cal whistled. "You're doing heroin now?"

"Apparently." After another swallow, Nick wiped his mouth with the back of his hand. "I walked in on a man trying to drug and kidnap a young woman." He rubbed his jaw. "The ass clocked me pretty good. Pulled a gun."

"Fuck. You called the police?"

"Yes. The club's out in Brookline. Well out of your jurisdiction, I'm certain. But you'll hear about it in the morning. The club owner...something's off about him. He doesn't know a fucking thing about BDSM other than what he's read on the internet, and his staff Masters are jokes."

Cal made a contemplative noise. "What's the name of the club?"

"Bound."

"Shit." After a sigh, Cal paused for so long, Nick blinked hard to clear his vision to make sure the call hadn't dropped. When he continued, Nick almost lost his hold on his rocks glass. "Nick, I'm leading a joint task force—five districts. Bound is one of the clubs we're investigating. We suspect a few of the clubs around Boston are serving as grooming grounds for sex trafficking by the Russian mob."

Nick choked on his next sip of scotch. "Shite. Really?"

Cal groaned over the line. "That's the problem. I don't know. This isn't my world, Nick. I've got a government official claiming his daughter's been kidnapped. Her best friend says she was into BDSM and had gone to Bound a week before she disappeared. Then another dance club called Pure Black a few days later. But all of the evidence my guys have found leads me to believe that she just took off because her parents were pushing her towards law school and she wanted to be a musician."

"Did you investigate Bound on your own?" Nick rubbed his eyes as he thought back over his few hours at the sex club. Had he missed something? Accents? Untoward glances beyond the standard lewd looks the men often gave the women?

"Of course. What kind of cop do you think I am?"

"The kind who stays out of bars and clubs," Nick replied. "And the most vanilla man on the bloody planet."

Cal laughed, his indignation fading. "That I may be, but my guys practically scream 'cop.' Doesn't matter if they're dressed head-to-toe in black leather and chains or a three-piece suit. The only good undercover guys I've got right now are tied up on another case. I hate to ask. But...would you consider going back? You understand that lifestyle. Hell, you live it. You won't stand out."

"You do know who I am, yeah?" Nick stared at his empty glass. Another? Why the hell not? "I stand out, Cal. Alex may be the more recognizable Fairhaven these days but after tonight? The press is going to be on my ass unless my lawyer can work miracles. I can see the headlines now. 'What's disgraced billionaire Nicholas Fairhaven up to?' That sort of shite." His words slurred as he poured more whiskey.

"How much have you had to drink?" Cal's voice became sharper as his authoritative lieutenant persona pushed to the surface. "Maybe I should come over."

"Not enough. And no. I'm not in danger of relapsing tonight. Before I called, maybe. Not anymore. The drink quiets the memories. Once I go to bed, it'll be done for another year."

"Nick, grief is a dangerous emotion. It makes us do things we'd never think of otherwise. Promise me one thing."

He didn't want to promise a damn thing, but Cal had saved his life—more than once. "What?"

"If you even think of placing a bet, you call me back. I don't care what time it is or what I'm doing. And we're going to a meeting tomorrow."

"Yeah. Fine. I'll meet you at seven." Nick tossed back the last of his drink. "And I'm not going back to Bound, Cal. If I do, my brother might never speak to me again. Now, if there's nothing else, I'd like to get on with it, yeah?"

Cal mumbled, "Fine. Drink a couple of glasses of water, will ya?"

"Maybe." Nick jabbed the screen to end the call, but then

stared at the phone in his hand for so long, by the time he returned his gaze to his glass, all of the ice had melted. Perhaps another drink wasn't such a good idea.

"I'm sorry, darling," he whispered to Lia's memory, just out of reach. "I hope you're at peace now."

# 5

Nick

A LITTLE AFTER 8:00 a.m., Nick rapped on his brother's front door.
He'd slept poorly—the alcohol hadn't helped—and he wanted to
forget the past twenty-four hours. Except for Sofia. The one
bright spot in an otherwise awful day. Within a few seconds,
Samuel, Alex's majordomo, answered the door. "Good morning,
sir. Mr. Fairhaven is in his study. Can I offer you coffee?"

"No, Samuel. Thank you." Nick strode towards Alex's home
office without removing his coat. He had a feeling he wouldn't be
staying long.

His brother looked up when he entered, and Nick read the
frustration and disappointment in Alex's eyes. Rushing to stop
the tirade that would quickly follow, he held up his hand. "Ben is
filing an injunction against the *Babbler* as we speak. Phone
cameras are the single worst invention of the modern age."

Alex vibrated with anger. "They accused you of letting that
girl overdose. Why else would you be photographed with an
unconscious woman and a syringe, Nicholas? At a BDSM club,
no less. I realize our sexual preferences aren't a secret, but that

doesn't mean we should flaunt them in front of the whole world."
Alex sank back in his chair and scrubbed his face with his hands.
"I've spent the past hour trying to placate the board. You're lucky
they haven't already filed a motion to sever all ties with you. If
this story gains any traction, releasing our quarterly financials
won't give us the stock price boost we've been counting on."

"Can I talk now?" Nick dropped into a chair across from Alex.
"I've never touched a damn thing stronger than scotch, and you
know it."

"Until last night?"

"Stop interrupting." Though Alex had three inches and fifty
pounds on him—all of it muscle—Nick didn't have any qualms
about using his extra five years of life against his brother. "Terrance dragged me out last night. You know what day it was. And
yet, you didn't bother to call."

Alex flinched. "Elizabeth wasn't feeling well. I couldn't
leave her."

"You couldn't have picked up the fucking phone?" Alexander's
ambivalence towards the worst day of Nick's year—of his life—
didn't sit well, but after a moment, he processed his brother's
words. "Is Elizabeth okay?"

Alexander's wife helped bridge the tense relationship
between the two brothers, and though Nick had largely stayed
away of late, she still called to check up on him from time to time.
In her, Nick had found a sympathetic ear, and above all, understanding. She'd even softened Alex—most of the time.

"Her father had a heart attack. A week ago. She only found
out yesterday." Venom infused Alex's tone, and Nick thought he
heard his brother's teeth grind together. "I've sent a private inves-
tigator to try to find out more information and the jet is on
standby."

"Fuck me. I'm sorry, Alex. If there's anything I can do—"

"You can stay out of the bloody news." Alex's phone buzzed,
and he glanced down at the screen. "Explain. Quickly."

When Nick finished recounting the events of the previous night, Alex sighed. "Get the real story out today, Nicholas. And for fuck's sake, if you can get the girl to give a statement, do so."

This time, when Alex's phone rang, he jabbed the screen. "Yes?" After a moment, he covered the microphone with his hand. "I need to take this. Fix this cock-up and let me know when it's done."

Nick slunk out of his brother's office feeling more like a chastised teenager than the forty-one-year-old heir to a billion-dollar fortune.

**Sofia**

"Have you seen my student ID?" Sofia dumped her backpack out on the kitchen counter and cursed as her lip gloss and highlighters clattered onto the floor and rolled away. "Gina! Get your ass out here and help me. I'm going to be late for my exam."

With a yawn, Sofia's younger sister trudged into the kitchen. A lipstick smear trailed along the corner of her mouth, and bloodshot eyes blinked slowly in an attempt to focus. "It's too early," she whined as she tried to straighten her robe. "Have a heart, Sis."

"You're the one who stayed out until 4:00 a.m. and then came in like a heard of elephants." Sofia thrust her hand deep into her backpack, rooting around desperately. "You borrowed my ID again, didn't you?"

"I needed the Apple store discount." Gina pulled a shiny new iPhone from the pocket of her robe. "I can't very well backpack across Switzerland with a four-year-old phone, now can I?"

Heading for the coffee pot, Gina poured herself a cup and leaned against the counter.

*She's leaving soon. Don't lose it.*

Despite herself, Sofia clenched her hands into fists and leveled a glare at her sister. "What did you do with my ID? I can't take my exam without it."

"Don't get your panties in a bunch. I'll find it."

"Now," Sofia snapped as her sister lifted the mug to her lips. "If I don't leave in the next five minutes, it won't matter. Professor Ott won't let me in the door if I'm late."

As Gina disappeared back into her bedroom, Sofia grumbled and shoved her book, notebook, and wallet into her backpack. Where had she gone wrong with her sister? For ten years, she'd taken care of Gina. Hell, she'd given up her own dreams so Gina could go to school and not worry about working. Would a little less attitude be too much to ask?

"Gina! I swear, if I fail this test because of you..."

With a sigh, Gina leaned against the door jamb and held out the student ID. "Relax, Sis. One ID. Safe and sound."

Snatching her precious identification from her sister's outstretched hand, Sofia bolted out the door. It'd be a miracle if she made it to her test on time.

Panting, her shoulder aching from the heavy load and the long run across the quad, Sofia swiped her student ID across the building's card reader. The halls were packed. She bobbed and wove through the throng of students before skidding to a halt as Professor Ott started to pull the classroom door closed. "Wait! Please!"

Pushing sixty, the tall woman with a crown of gray hair raised a brow. "Cutting it rather close, aren't you Miss Oliviera?"

"The T...was packed," she gasped as she pointed at the clock on the classroom wall. "I'm still on time."

"Barely." The professor sighed, then stepped back to let Sofia through the door. "Take your seat and begin."

At the end of the exam, Sofia let her head hit the desk with a solid *thunk*. She'd studied for a week, yet her brain felt like Swiss cheese. Or perhaps a waterlogged sponge, incapable of soaking up a single additional fact.

"Miss Oliviera?" Professor Ott stood over her with a stack of tests cradled in her arms. "I probably don't have to tell you that you're skating by with a C average. Is this test going to be more of the same?"

Sofia's eyes burned. "Maybe. There was a problem at my job last night. I didn't get home until after 2:00 a.m. But I've been studying all week."

"You have excellent instincts, my dear. But I'm afraid that's all they are at the moment. Instincts. If you're serious about being a family counselor, you have to make your studies a priority."

With a nod, Sofia slipped her pen into her bag and pushed to her feet. "I'll have at least a full week off before the final to do nothing but study. I have to pass this class."

"See that you do," the professor said. "When I wrote your recommendation letter for Boston College, I told them you were one of the brightest students I'd had the pleasure of teaching in years. But these last few months...I don't know where that young woman went."

"Bills," Sofia whispered as Professor Ott strode away. "She had to pay the bills."

Unable to hold onto her composure, Sofia turned and fled from the room.

Anger clouded her vision, and as she shoved through the students milling around the campus entrance, she ran right into a trim brick wall.

"Shit." Sofia tried to pull away, but the wall had arms and steadied her.

Nick's frosty blue eyes warmed as his lips curved into a smile. "There you are. Given the size of this place, and the fact you didn't give me your number or your last name, I worried I wouldn't find you."

"You showed up." She couldn't manage much more. Not with the lump in her throat and the tears of frustration lining her eyes.

"Why wouldn't I? We had plans, did we not?" Nick held her at arm's length, and when a single tear tumbled onto her cheek, he reached up and brushed it away. "What's wrong? You look knack-ered, love."

The kind words, along with his tone—one that said he was the sort of man who took care of others—sent her careening to the edge of control. "I...uh...my test..."

Understanding softened his features. "Are you going home after this?"

The question shocked her enough to answer without think-ing. "Yes."

Nick wrapped an arm around her. "There's a coffee shop not too far from your apartment that I'm rather fond of. I'll understand if you're not up for that snack you mentioned, but may I at least buy you a cup of coffee?"

She didn't agree so much as not protest as he guided her down the street, but somewhere under the tears and shock, she relished in the feeling of being tended to, even though she barely knew the man. "You don't have to—"

"I'm afraid I didn't sleep well last night. I could use the caffeine," he said with a chuckle. Around the corner on a side street, headlights on a silver Audi flashed once. Nick held the passenger door open for her, and she sank into the buttery, leather seat.

The car smelled like him, and Sofia let her head fall back against the headrest as she tried to force Professor Ott's disappointed expression from her memories. "I think I failed the test," she murmured as he started the car. "Or I came close. Fuck."

"Are you sure?"

They pulled out into traffic, the car purring to life so quietly that she felt the engine more than heard it. "Pretty sure. I couldn't concentrate. My sister got home at 4:00 a.m. She's not...quiet. The guy she hooked up with—ugh. They were going at it for two hours."

"Will that make it difficult for you to pass the class?"

Sofia didn't want to think about that possibility. If she didn't pass, she could kiss her Master's program goodbye. Instead, she closed her eyes and tried not to let her emotions get the better of her.

Despite the mid-morning hour, traffic ground to a halt, and Nick glanced over at her. "We've got a bit of a ride. Recline the seat. Close your eyes if you want."

Sofia raised a brow. "I met you last night. At a BDSM club. You may be famous, but I'm not stupid."

A rich laugh bellowed through his chest. "No. You're not. I could be a murderer and simply have enough money to cover my tracks. Though if that were the case, the police wouldn't have questioned me for so long last night."

"Point taken." She ran a hand through her messy curls, wishing she'd had time for at least a little makeup today. "I should text Gina, though."

"We're going to a coffee shop called 'Artist's Grind.' It's on Houston Street. You'll be home by one at the latest. And give her my phone number." Nick rattled off the seven digits, and Sofia sent the text, a little surprised at Nick's sensitivity.

"You're not what I expected." His brows arched and she gave him a small shake of her head. "I mean...I always imagined rich and powerful men just...did what they wanted. You're going out of your way to make sure I'm comfortable."

"If you'd prefer, I could start barking orders at you. But I much prefer a gentler approach. My brother does enough barking for the both of us. Case in point: this morning. I'm afraid he's still quite upset with me."

Something in his voice said his morning had gone about as well as hers. "Over the news stories?"

"My lawyer is trying to get them retracted, but the damage has been done."

They lapsed into silence for the rest of the drive, Sofia staring out the window as the city crawled by. When he pulled off the freeway, she smiled. "I love this part of town. All the little shops. I rarely get down here."

"My brother's wife discovered this little coffee shop. She's friends with the owner," Nick explained. "When I left my job, I started coming here once a week or so. Though I got out of the habit. I'm not sure why." Again, an odd note laced his tone, and Sofia was surprised that the famous billionaire seemed to be so unsure of himself.

Once they'd parked, Nick opened her door and offered her his arm. His manners left her off balance. She was touched that he was such a gentleman and uncomfortable with being treated so...delicately. Outside of Artist's Grind, he glanced down at her, hope in his eyes. "Shall we?"

When she nodded, he held the door, and Sofia ducked inside the cozy little shop. A petite brunette behind the counter greeted them with a smile. "I haven't seen you lately, Nicholas."

"I'm sorry, Devan. I've been"—he shifted on his feet—"trying to keep a low profile."

Devan nodded, her bright eyes dimming slightly. "I suppose that's for the best. Who's your friend?"

"This is Sofia..." Nick frowned. "I'm sorry, my dear, but you never told me your last name."

"Oliviera." Sofia's cheeks heated. What must Devan think of her walking in with a man who didn't even know her last name? Nick flinched as if he'd just realized his gaffe.

Turning to Devan, he shook off the dark cloud that had settled over him. "Could I have an Americano? And whatever Sofia would like?"

"Cappuccino?" She wanted to escape, to run away and lose herself in a movie for a few hours, eat a bucket of popcorn, forget about her failed test, her sister leaving town soon, her upcoming shift at Bound where she'd spend the entire night worrying about the attempted kidnapping and whether she would be safe walking to the T after work—everything. But bolting from the coffee shop wouldn't solve anything, and she did need the caffeine. Plus, something about Nick drew her in, and she wanted to find out more about him.

"Coming right up," Devan said as she turned to the coffee grinder. "Anything to eat?"

Nick cringed. "I should have offered. Devan makes some of the best scones in Boston. What would you like?"

The pastry case overflowed with all sorts of delicious offerings, and Sofia's stomach rumbled. "Um, the cheddar biscuit?"

Nick laid a twenty on the counter once he'd ordered his scone, led Sofia over to one of the bistro tables, and pulled out a chair for her. "Please, sit. Coffee will fix...well, not everything, but it will certainly help both of us."

"Why did you ask me out?" She sniffled, the change in temperature from the brisk, spring morning to the warm coffee shop making her nose run. Cursing as she dug around in her bag for a tissue and came up empty, her breath hitched when Nick offered her his silk handkerchief.

"It's clean, I promise you." He smiled and damn if her insides didn't tremble for a brief moment. "And I'm buying you a cup of coffee because last night was awful for both of us, you look like you've had a shite day, and that...bothers me."

Sofia took the silk and dabbed at her nose. "You don't know me."

"No. I don't. But despite what the press likes to report, I'm not a complete ass. Plus, I need a little information about Bound."

Oh God. *Had* he been there to gamble? And was that why he'd asked her out? "Information?"

"For a friend. After I spoke to him last night, he asked me a few questions about the club. I thought perhaps I could get those answers from you, rather than that dick of a boss of yours who doesn't know what's going on at his own club."

Her hands shook as she folded the silk into a tight square. "You're pretty observant."

"Comes with the lifestyle," Nick said simply.

"Oh." Of course. A man like Nick Fairhaven wasn't a sub in any universe. And though Sofia hadn't played in years, working at Bound, she could spot the attentive, caring Doms as easily as the ones who weren't.

Devan brought over their drinks and snacks, and Nick touched her arm. "Thank you, Devan. Business going well?"

"More or less. Mac hasn't been able to work much lately, though. He had to have another surgery. I need a vacation. I think we're going to close for a week once he recovers and do some-thing...relaxing. Spend a week on a beach somewhere."

"You deserve it." Nick watched the woman walk away, a frown marring his handsome features. "She runs this place by herself. In two years, she's never taken a day off—from what I've heard." He shook his head, then returned his focus to Sofia. After a taste of her cappuccino, the velvety foam sticking to her top lip, she rushed to hide behind her napkin before speaking. "So... you're...last night at Bound, you were there to..."

"I'm a Master, Sofia. A Dominant." He took a sip of his Americano and then sighed. "Though I haven't played in eighteen months, nor did I have any intention of playing last night." Resting his forearm on the table, he leaned forward. "You never answered my question in the car. Will this morning's exam hurt your chances to pass this class?"

Sofia choked on a sound halfway between a laugh and a sob. "If I don't ace the final—and find some extra credit points, I could lose my spot in the Master's program. I've worked every damn day for the past ten years to put my sister through school, make a life for us. And I'm about to throw it all away with less than three weeks left in the semester." She shook her head. "If I do fail the test, I'm going to have to quit. Though at least Gina won't be banging around at all hours soon."

"Your sister? How old is she?"

"Twenty-three," Sofia said as she tried to force her spine a little straighter. Here in this quiet shop, Nick relaxed, and she wondered what he did for fun. Then again, she wondered what *she* did for fun. "Gina's brilliant. And headed for a backpacking trip through Switzerland in ten days, then off to Germany on a full scholarship to study some algae species that only exists in one specific lake no one's ever heard of." Taking a sip of her cappuccino to force the lump in her throat to go the fuck away, she clutched Nick's handkerchief in her free hand.

He leaned forward, concern drawing his brows together. "Your words say you want her to go, but your tone says otherwise."

"Gina isn't my biggest fan. I had to be Mom for so long, that's all she sees in me. But it's been just us for years...and she's my sister. I love her. Even if she doesn't feel the same." Sofia tried to keep her lower lip from wobbling as she thought about how lonely and quiet the apartment would be without her sister's huge personality taking up space.

Nick chuckled. "You know I have a brother. We've spent most of our lives hating one another. As I recall, at twenty-three, Alex told me to sod off in front of our mother, then punched me in the face." A smile accompanied the memory, and Sofia caught a whiff of sandalwood and cloves as he ran a hand through his unruly blond locks. "I, being five years older and infinitely wiser, did nothing. Mum kicked him out of the house and told him he couldn't return until he could be a proper gentleman and apologize."

"How long did it take?" The tension in Sofia's shoulders started to melt away, and she leaned back in the chair, cupping the coffee mug in her chilled fingers.

"For Alex to apologize?" Nick glanced down at his watch. "We're going on thirteen years, six months, four days, and perhaps nineteen hours?" At Sofia's laugh, he continued, "Mum relented when he returned with her favorite pastries from the local baker. We may not be the closest of siblings, but we love one another. I'm certain Gina doesn't hate you."

They didn't speak for several minutes. As the coffee soothed Sofia's raw nerves, she tried to remember the little she'd seen in the papers about Nick Fairhaven over the years. A brutal negotiator, yet a good businessman. Then some trouble with the mob. Vague memories of the reports of his gambling problem. Despite hating Victor and wanting nothing to do with his illegal poker game, she *had* to know if that had been the reason for his visit. "You said your friend dragged you out last night. And you promised to tell me why you wanted to get drunk."

A shadow darkened his eyes, and he fiddled with his shirt

collar. "I lost someone very special to me. Eight years ago last night. Terrance didn't want me to be alone, and for some reason, thought a BDSM club was the proper environment for me to... forget my troubles."

"So you *were* there to play."

"I was there to appease Terrance only. I don't share, Sofia. Nor do I enjoy being a target of voyeurs. Any play I engage in will be in the privacy of my bedroom—or hers." As he spoke, he cocked his head. "What about you? You said you don't date, but are you... attached to a Dom?"

Sofia nearly choked on her cappuccino. "Um...no. And...how did you know I'm..."

"You're a natural submissive, love. When *did* you last play?" He lifted his cup, and she couldn't help watching his every movement as he sipped, then licked his lips. "Sofia?"

*Shit. Get yourself together.* A bit of foam molded to her lips as she gulped down enough of the caffeinated courage to respond to him, and she hastily swiped at her mouth with a napkin before responding. "Five years ago. I...had a boyfriend, and he was a practicing Dom. But then Gina had to transfer out of the dorms to save money, and I let her move in with me. That sort of put a damper on the relationship with my former Master. I haven't been with anyone since. Haven't dated or played."

Streaks of aquamarine glowed in the azure depths of his eyes as he leaned forward. "Would you like to?"

# 6

## Nick

ACROSS FROM HIM, Sofia squirmed in her chair. *Oh, she'd be such a delightful sub,* he thought with a smile. "My apologies, love. I didn't mean to make you uncomfortable." Except he had. Something about the exotic beauty called him in a way he'd not felt in years.

"I'm not looking to date anyone," she said quietly. "Once I finish this class, I start full time at Boston College. After my first year, I'll get a paid internship—it's part of the Master's program. If I fail...well, then I'll be stuck at Bound. Damnit. I guess I can't march into Victor's office tonight and quit after all." Sofia stared into her cappuccino, and Nick found himself mesmerized by the way her lower lip jutted out slightly to one side as she worried the plump flesh between her teeth.

"Would you consider another bartending job? I know a few restaurant owners. I could...put in a good word for you." The offer escaped before he could stop himself, and she flinched. *Or not.*

"Thank you, Nick. Really," she said as she met his gaze. Her dark brown eyes still carried the strain of a long, late night. Underneath the exhaustion, however, a sparkle of determination lingered. "I'll be fine. I've been tending bar for seven years. Never had anything but glowing reviews—until Victor. If I have to find another job, any of my old bosses would vouch for me." She took a bite of her biscuit, and her eyelids fluttered. "Oh God. This is fantastic."

"I wouldn't steer you wrong. Not where food is concerned." He sat back, letting the coffee settle his nerves after the tense conversation with Alex. Though, Sofia's presence probably had more to do with the deep contentment that filled him rather than the caffeine. "Would you consider sharing a full meal sometime?"

"I..." Staring down at her hands clasped around her mug, she took a slow breath. When she raised her head, confusion clouded her gaze. "If it's too personal a question, ignore me. But who did you lose?"

Nick didn't answer right away.

"I'm sorry, I shouldn't have asked."

With a sad smile, he shook his head. "No, that's not it. I assume you're asking, in part, because a man in mourning shouldn't look to start something with another woman."

"Well...the thought did cross my mind. But you also promised to tell me why you were out last night, and you glossed over any sort of detailed answer." Taking a sip of her cappuccino, she inclined her head. "If I'm not mistaken, you've barely touched your coffee. I don't really understand why we're here—beyond you wanting to somehow make up for my terrible day that you had nothing to do with—but I'd rather talk than sit here in silence."

Nick tried not to let himself gape at the lovely, intelligent woman across from him. He was in trouble. Sofia had the power to captivate him and never let him go. Pulling himself out of his own thoughts, he swallowed hard over the lump in his throat. "Her name was Lia. We dated for three years, and she wore my collar for two—the only commitment I was mature enough to give her at the time. She died eight years ago. Last night was the anniversary of her death. I've healed—as much as one can after losing a loved one, I suppose—but April nineteenth is always a hard day for me. The last few years...I've spent it drunk and losing my shirt at the track. Last year and this year...well, betting is no longer an option. So drunk wins."

A hint of relief warmed her eyes. Sofia reached across the table and covered his hand with hers. "I'm sorry, Nick. For prying and for your loss."

The warmth in her fingers calmed him. "She gave me many things in our time together. Though I didn't realize it until recently, the most important gift was the knowledge that life is fragile. We can end in a heartbeat. How many twenty-six-year-old women develop stage four liver cancer? Less than fifty per year. I asked you out today because life is too short not to try to get to know someone you find interesting."

"Once my parents died, and I had to provide for myself and Gina, I started working at least two jobs—all the time. I haven't had more than a couple days off a row in years. And even then...I felt guilty the whole time." Her voice carried a deep longing as she glanced over at the cheery clock hanging on the wall behind the counter. "I wish I could stay longer. But if I leave now, I might be able to catch a couple of hours of sleep before my shift tonight."

Sofia stood and glanced down at his handkerchief still clutched in her hand. "I should wash this," she said, almost to herself.

"No need." His words escaped rougher than he intended and he kicked himself for letting his desire for her overwhelm his rational mind. "Bugger. I'm sorry. I just meant that I have others. And...you could return it to me another time."

An odd mix of arousal and fear flashed across her delicate features. "Thank you. For this and the coffee. It was nice to talk to you outside the club." She extended her free hand, offering him a friendly handshake.

"Have dinner with me?" He rose as well, catching her wrist and then rubbing his thumb over the soft flesh of her pulse point. "Tomorrow night."

"That wouldn't be a good idea." With a quick glance down at her boots, she shook her head. "We don't live in the same world, Nick."

"What world do I live in?" He kept his grip firm, but easily breakable. When she didn't pull away, he took a step closer. "I'm the black sheep of my family, Sofia. Lost most of my fortune last year. Hell, I don't even have a job at the moment. And after last night—I'm not sure I have a *world* any longer."

Nick cursed his words as they left his mouth. He wasn't poor, and he was building back his fortune day by day, but for now, he lived simply, with only a few splurges. Yet Sofia had just admitted she was scraping by, hand to mouth, and he sounded like a pompous ass. Of course she wouldn't want to go out with him.

Her threadbare coat—high quality, but obviously at least ten years old—a thin patch on the knee of her jeans, and a purse that had seen better days spoke of a highly resourceful, yet frugal woman.

"You still have a world. You're still rich. Still a Fairhaven. And I...have a sister and bills and an asshole boss and studying." She offered him an apologetic smile. "Dinner would be a bad idea."

"Don't decide now." Nick released his hold, then dipped his hand into his back pocket. From his wallet, he withdrew a business card—though it was woefully outdated. "Devan, can I borrow a pen?" He strode over to the counter, and when she slid a pen over to him, he thanked her with a smile.

Crossing out his former title, he scribbled what he hoped was a humorous replacement on the front, then flipped the card over and pursed his lips. Once he'd finished the quick note, he turned to find Sofia only two feet away. "Will you do me a favor?"

"Maybe," she said, hesitant.

"Call me tomorrow. If only to let me know how you're doing. Give me the opportunity to ask you to dinner one more time. I promise I won't pester you after that." He raised his brows as he held out the card and said a quick little prayer to himself.

Whether too polite to refuse or genuinely interested, he couldn't tell, but she accepted the card and tucked it quickly into her pocket. "All right. I should go. Thank you again for the coffee." She rushed towards the door, and as she tugged on the handle, he thought he heard her add, "And the company."

**Sofia**

Sofia hurried down the street, her focus on the round T-station sign at the end of the block. The caffeine thrummed through her veins, and her hands shook as she dug out her fare card and swiped it across the turnstile reader. The race down the escalator, across the platform, and through the subway car doors a second before they closed left her heart pounding, and she collapsed into one of the well-worn seats before she let herself think back to what had just happened in the coffee shop.

Nick Fairhaven had come on to her. Worse, he'd asked her out on a *date*. What the hell was he thinking? She frowned at the small bulge under her sweater where her stomach decided to muffin-top over her jeans. She wasn't heavy, but she had ample curves, unlike Gina, who could easily model size zero clothing.

Her hand went to her messy locks, tucking a particularly unruly curl behind her ear. Of all the days to forego a shower. And he'd still looked at her like he wanted to eat her for dinner. *Of course. He saw me in my uniform last night.* The tight corset and micro-miniskirt left very little to the imagination. Sofia would disappoint him rather quickly once he realized that the sexiest item of clothing in her wardrobe at the moment was a single little black dress that had seen better days. Everything else? Jeans, leggings, yoga pants, t-shirts, sweaters...nothing clingy or revealing. When she got off of work, all she wanted to do was cover up.

"Get over it," she muttered to herself. "He'll forget all about you by tomorrow."

She wouldn't forget about him, though. Not the way he smelled, or how safe she'd felt tucked under his arm. How long had it been since someone had taken care of her? Too long.

As she emerged from the T-station a few blocks from her apartment, her phone buzzed.

*Gina: Where are you? I thought you were going to pick up some travel-sized containers for my shampoo and stuff?*

Tears pricked Sofia's eyes, and she fumbled for the silk she'd tucked in her pocket. As she dabbed her cheeks, she caught his scent, and damn if she didn't regret running away from him. "You were wrong about my sister, Nick," she said quietly. "And you're wrong about me, too."

Straightening her shoulders, she blew out a deep breath. *Pull yourself together, babe. The only one who can take care of you is you.*

By the time she got home from her unplanned excursion to the drugstore, a headache banded around her skull. All dreams of a nap faded when she saw the clothing bomb Gina detonated. Blouses, sweaters, skirts, and all sorts of unmentionables were strewn over every surface of the living room. Sofia slept on the pull-out couch, and the living room was her bedroom. As such, her *bed* was currently occupied—by a tall, brown-haired guy wearing a muscle shirt and torn jeans.

"Gina?" she called as she dropped her backpack on the counter. The guy glanced up, but then his phone beeped, and he returned his focus to the screen without a single word.

Her sister's straight black hair dripped water all over the floor as she poked her head out of the bedroom. "Oh. You're back. Great. Did you pick up the stuff I needed?"

"I'm not your maid. But yes. I did." She handed over the small bag and cursed herself. If she didn't want Gina to think of her as a maid, she needed to stop acting like one. "Any chance you could dump all this stuff in your own room?" Gesturing to the couch and the guy lounging on the well-worn cushions, Sofia tried—and failed—to keep the "mom" tone from her voice.

"Um. I really need to figure out what I'm donating to Goodwill. I'll be done by the time you get home from work tonight."

Sofia wrapped her arm around Gina's shoulders and urged her into the bedroom. "I slept all of four hours last night, baby girl. Plus, I'm pretty sure I failed my exam. Please? Can you and the phone-obsessed bodybuilder out there clear out until five?"

"This is my place too." Gina's petulant tone grated on Sofia's nerves and she blew out a slow, controlled breath. "Look, in a couple of weeks, you won't have to deal with me anymore, Sis. I'm sorry, but I have to fit my entire life into one suitcase and a backpack and going through all of this stuff takes time. I thought you'd understand."

"And the guy?"

Gina's eyes sparkled as tried to stifle a giggle. "Rick's great. I met him down at the student union." She lowered her voice. "Might as well have a little fun before I leave town."

"I thought...we could spend some time together." Though they'd never seen eye-to-eye, Sofia didn't want her sister living halfway around the world for the next four years. Not truly. Why couldn't she have applied for a grant in New York City? Or Washington D.C.? Germany...Sofia would never be able to afford a trip to Germany. Her eyes burned as Gina ran a hand through her still-damp locks.

"Look, I love you, Sof. But this is the last bit of...freedom I have before I'm going to be chained to a desk for the rest of my natural life. I'm going to enjoy every minute. We'll do dinner on Sunday night. Hell, I'll make sure I'm free after four. Drinks, dinner, and maybe we can even go dancing, okay?"

Shoving the regret and hurt down deep where the emotions couldn't hurt her, Sofia nodded. "Okay. Do me a favor, though. Keep Rick in your room until after I've showered and dressed?"

"Will do." Gina skipped into the living room, grabbed Rick's hand, and led him back to the bedroom. The ass still didn't bother to acknowledge Sofia.

Twelve days. Twelve days until her sister would fly away and Sofia would finally be alone. She couldn't decide how she'd feel about saying goodbye.

## 7

## Nick

NICK SHOVED his hands into his pockets as he strode down Cambridge Street. The little hole-in-the-wall place Cal favored was hidden away down a side alley, and he ducked his head against the wind that blew through the narrow gap between the old brick buildings.

"Corner Cafe" glowed in bright neon, the sign taking up the top half of a single lit window. From the looks of the place, they'd be the only two diners all evening. Probably because the cafe didn't serve alcohol and had all of five menu items.

Cal unfolded his bulky frame from the booth as Nick approached and offered a firm handshake. "Doing all right?" he asked.

Frowning, Nick unbuttoned his coat. "Better than I'll be after this meal. Do you have a personal vendetta against vegetables? Or anything that's not fried?"

With a rolling laugh, Cal slapped Nick's back, the distinct scent of stale coffee on his breath and the overwhelming aroma of Christmas trees from his cologne enveloping Nick. "Live a little, will ya? Fish and chips never killed anyone."

"If only what they served here could be called *chips*. Or fish, for that matter." Nick glanced over the menu, his momentary hope that Corner Cafe might have learned how to spell—or added something green to their menu—disappearing as the server approached their table.

"Just a bowl of your chowder," Nick said after Cal had ordered his usual monster plate of food. The man was pushing sixty but rarely looked his age. Today, though, bags swelled under his bloodshot eyes, and his skin carried a sickly gray tone. "You, my friend, look like you're a bit shattered. And since you don't drink..."

Cal rubbed the back of his thick neck. "It's this damn case. I looked into that attempted kidnapping you told me about."

"And?"

"The girl, Emily Norse, checked herself out of the hospital this morning. But she doesn't remember much—if anything—about the attack. Just being scared, a man's voice, some sort of accent."

"Shite, Cal. *I* have an accent. Not all that thick anymore, but..." Nick sucked down half of his water to soothe the lump in his throat. He'd hoped once the police—or the press—talked to the girl, Ben would have legal grounds to sue the *Babbler* for all they were worth. He'd caught a photographer tailing him after he left Artist's Grind.

*I should warn Sofia in case they saw her with me.*

That would be just his luck. Finding an intelligent, beautiful submissive and then having her scared off by the press. His momentary worry faded when Cal sighed and ran a hand through his thinning white hair. "Listen, man. Can I call in a favor?"

Pursing his lips, Nick met Cal's gaze. "You pulled me out of a free-fall, mate. You and Hannah opened your home when I couldn't stand to be in my own flat because of all the memories."

"That's what sponsors are for."

He and Cal fell silent as the server delivered their meals, and when Cal jabbed a piece of fried fish the size of a deck of cards, Nick leaned forward. "What do you need?"

"Go back to Bound. Look around for me. If I don't figure out who's taking these girls, my captain is going to bust me down to beat cop." He rubbed his rather sizable gut. "That'll kill me."

Though he had no desire to ever set foot in the BDSM club again, he couldn't deny his sponsor anything. Even if it did mean he'd have to face his brother's wrath. "I'll go back later tonight. But I need to go to a meeting first."

"That's why we're here." Cal toasted Nick with his water. "The YMCA's only two blocks over. If we don't order dessert, we'll make it."

"This place serves dessert? Is it fried?" Nick dragged his spoon through something that no self-respecting New England cafe would ever call chowder, grimaced, and tried a single spoonful. Awful.

Dipping his hand into his pocket, Nick ran a finger over the eighteen-month chip. Sofia's smile and sweet scent invaded his memories. If nothing else, he'd get to see her again, and that single thought soothed the demons inside him.

The basement of the YMCA smelled like cheap coffee and old doughnuts. Same as every single meeting Nick had ever been to. Once, in a fit of desperation, he'd found a meeting in an airport lounge in Los Angeles, and even that room carried the same scent. Men and women filed in slowly, some chatting with one another, others looking around like they were frightened someone would recognize them.

Memories of his first meeting, scared out of his mind, floated to the surface. He'd stood outside the doors for half an hour trying to muster up the courage to step inside. Until Cal had found him.

*"Watching a meeting from outside won't do you any good, you know?" The big, burly cop shoved his hands into his pockets and stood shoulder-to-shoulder with Nick. "The first step is always the hardest."*

*"How do these things work?" Nick said. "You go in, tell everyone you've got a problem, and it just...gets easier?"*

*"Nope."*

*"You're not making me feel any better, mate."*

*The man next to him chuckled. "Recovery takes time. For some of us, it never gets easier. Me? I've got the gambling mostly licked. Super Bowl Sunday and the Derby are the only times I really struggle. But the drinking...shit. I think about having a drink almost every damn day."*

*"So what's the point? Why do you keep showing up?" Through the narrow slit in the door, Nick made out four rows of chairs, heads—men and women—some nodding, some perfectly still. "I haven't placed a bet in two weeks. And I feel so bloody empty inside. How is admitting that going to help?"*

*As he said the words, Nick's burden felt a little lighter. The older gentleman next to him chuckled. "You should see your face, buddy. You ready to go in now?"*

*"I...yeah. I guess I am." Nick held out his hand. "Do...are we supposed to be anonymous?"*

*"First names only. Not that folks won't know who you are. I'm Cal." The man offered a firm handshake, followed by a clap on the back. "Let's go in. It's been a while since I stood up and told my story. I can show you how it's done."*

Now, he and Cal sat in the back of the room, listening to a woman in her fifties talk about losing her entire family after spending their life savings playing online poker. When she finished, and the moderator asked for volunteers, Nick stood. "I'd like a few minutes, Brian."

"Come on up and introduce yourself."

Nick gripped the edges of the well-worn podium, his palms damp. "I'm Nick." He held up his hand to silence the customary "Hello, Nick" chorus that usually followed an introduction. "I try to share my story every couple of months because some days, talking about it is the only thing that stops me from placing a bet."

A few nods from the audience gave Nick enough courage to continue. "I started gambling because I lost someone precious to me." His voice cracked, and he searched out Cal's face in the audience. "Well, that's not entirely correct. Her death didn't turn me into a gambler. When she died, a piece of my heart died too. The hole grew until I thought it would consume me. Then, one day, a friend took me to the track. The rush I got from winning a rather sizable bet made the pain go away for a short time. I forgot how lonely I was. How I had to go home every night to an empty house when I wanted to go home to her. That rush kept me going back, again and again and again until I came close to losing it all." Nick pulled his chip from his pocket. "I haven't placed a bet in nineteen months, fifteen days, and...probably two hours."

The audience clapped, and Nick ran a hand through his hair. "Some days, I don't feel the itch at all. Others, like yesterday, nothing quiets the demons. Except being here. Telling my story."

Another round of applause, which made Nick shift uncomfortably on his feet, and he nodded as he returned to his seat. For at least a few hours now, he'd be able to breathe. Just deep enough to make it through the rest of the day—and his upcoming trip back to Bound.

**Sofia**

As she slid a Fuzzy Navel—sans the vodka and schnapps—across the bar, Sofia tried to hide her wince. She bought these shoes because they claimed to have fantastic arch support, but three years of daily use and they felt like medieval torture devices.

"Smile," Victor barked in her ear as he pressed closer than necessary on his way to the other side of the bar. "No one's forcing you to be here, *сýка.*"

"*I'm* forcing myself to be here," she muttered under her breath once he'd stooped to unlock the special cabinet that held the hard stuff. There had to be a game tonight. Otherwise, he wouldn't be down here. The club only served alcohol once a week, on what was dubbed "hard limits" night. Those nights, only seasoned patrons were allowed in, and no matter how many times she'd asked, imagining the tips would be fantastic, Victor had never invited her to work one of those nights.

Tucking a bottle of whiskey under his arm and locking the cabinet, Victor stood and met Sofia's gaze. "You. Come upstairs."

"But...the bar—"

"Now. Leo will cover for you."

Why the hell was he inviting her up to the poker game now? She didn't want any part of his illegal activities. But with a full two hundred in her tip jar tonight, she wasn't going to do anything to get herself fired until the end of her shift. After that... maybe she could go back to living off of ramen and water and search for another job.

Victor led her down the hall and around a corner, then paused outside the locked door to the stairwell. Sliding open a panel in the wall, he punched in a ten digit code. The door popped open, and he gestured towards the stairs. "Up."

Victor pressed his large palm to her back and pushed her through the door. "You breathe one word of this to anyone, and you will regret it."

*I already regret coming in tonight.*

Nerves churned in her belly as she climbed the stairs with Victor close enough for her to feel the heat of him behind her. At the top of the stairs, she pushed open another door and tried to school her features into a calm mask.

At least two high-ranking city officials and a man wearing a badge and gun at his hip sat around the round table. Chips piled high in the center, and the room reeked of bourbon and vodka. "This is her?" the cop asked.

"Yes. She left with him last night." Victor prodded her forward. "She's needed at the bar. Ask your questions so she can get back to work."

*Nick. This is about Nick. Shit.*

Sofia tried not to look any of the men in the eyes; if it came down to it, being able to identify them probably wouldn't be healthy. But the cop pushed to his feet, towering over her.

"You know Nicholas Fairhaven."

"Y-yes. A little. Not well. I only met him last night." Sofia's voice wavered, and she tried not to take a step back.

"Nicholas Fairhaven used to be one of the biggest gamblers in the city. We want to know if he was here last night to join our game," a man she didn't want to believe was the mayor's chief of staff said.

"I wouldn't know."

Nick's words echoed in her head. *"I chose another vice. And I'm in recovery for that one.*

Sure, he could have lied. But the hurt in his eyes as he admitted his failings looked sincere. And then their conversation about the woman he'd lost... No. Nick Fairhaven had no desire to take part in Victor's illegal poker game.

The men scrutinized her and Sofia shifted on her feet, her shoes pinching her toes and sending a bone-deep ache through her calves. "I've had all of two conversations with Nick—Nicholas Fairhaven. If you want to know why he was here the other night, you'll have to ask him yourself."

Victor fastened his fingers around her arm tight enough to leave marks on someone without her Brazilian heritage.

"You're hurting me," she said through clenched teeth.

"My friend the captain," Victor said as he gestured to the cop, "says that you met Fairhaven for coffee today. So your pathetic excuses don't hold up. Next time you see him, find out if he's still gambling. And if he's not, what it would take to change that."

Sofia bristled, then wrenched her arm free. "I'm not your spy. I don't want any part of this." She turned to head for the door, but the cop stepped in front of her. His rumpled suit didn't do a thing to hide his broad shoulders and his breath stank of cheap whiskey.

"We need Nicholas Fairhaven to get involved in this game. You'll help us. Or I'm afraid you'll find yourself unemployed— and with an arrest record for stealing and drinking on the job that will show up on a background check for every bartending gig you apply in the future."

Sofia's eyes watered—both from the threat and the horrid stench of the man's hot breath in her face. "Please don't do this," she whispered. "He's...a nice guy. And he doesn't gamble anymore. Nothing I say is going to change that. I—"

"You'll think of something to say to convince him," the cop said.

"Go back to the bar," Victor spat. "And remember. We want him in the game. Soon."

Once the cop stepped aside, Sofia fled down the stairs,

holding her tears until she reached the bathroom, where she slumped against the sink and pulled Nick's handkerchief from inside her corset.

She was so fucked.

## 8

---

### Sofia

BACK AT THE bar and mostly composed, Sofia tried to ignore the warning bells in her head. *Quit now. Run as far as you can. Call Nick and tell him to stay the hell away from this place—and from you.*

But the steady stream of customers—tonight was newbie night—kept her busy enough that she could pretend nothing was wrong. Until she spotted a familiar blond head in the middle of the crowd.

"Oh shit. No." Scanning the bar, she said a little prayer of thanks as Leo returned from one of his many smoke breaks. "Cover for me," she said, pressing the latest drink ticket into his hand. "I need five minutes."

He glared at her, but turned towards the bottles behind him with a sigh and started mixing up a fruit-juice spritzer.

Even with her stupidly high heels, Sofia couldn't see over the crowd, and by the time she found Nick, he had almost made it to the bar. A smile curved his lips as he caught sight of her, but he must have read the panic on her face because he took her by the arms and bent his head close to her ear. "What's wrong, love?"

"Outside. Now." She wriggled free, grabbed his hand, and tugged him towards the door. They spilled out into the night and Sofia stumbled over an uneven piece of sidewalk. But Nick caught her, and for a brief moment, she relished being safe and protected. "You have to leave," she said into his shoulder.

"I wish I could. This is the last place I wanted to be tonight— well, inside the club at least. Right here, with you...I could be happy like this for quite a while." He tipped her head back with a gentle finger under her chin. "Why do you look like the world is ending?"

"I can't tell you. I just need you to leave. It's not...safe here." She cringed as the look in his eyes confirmed she'd said exactly the wrong thing. "I mean...for you. I'm safe. I'm fine. I promise."

"You're doing a poor job of convincing me, Sofia. Come home with me, and we can talk. Or we can go to a coffee shop. Tell your boss you're sick." Nick's blue eyes deepened, the whiskey-colored flecks flaring with the emotion in his tone.

She shook her head and wriggled free. "I don't have a choice. I have to stay. But...shit. Please. Trust me." Tears gathered in her eyes, and she swiped at the offending moisture with the back of her hand. "Forget about Bound. And me." An idea took hold. "There are reporters inside. Asking about you. If you go back in, the photos will be everywhere."

Nick narrowed his eyes at her, but when he spoke, his voice held a wary tone. "I'll go. But only if you promise to call me tomorrow."

Calling would lead to talking. And that would lead to more. She wanted the man in front of her. After so many years of denying her needs, she ached to see where this could go, whether they could have something, even if only a fling. Under his Henley, she'd felt his sculpted chest—not bulky, but lean, long muscles, lithe and strong.

"I can't, Nick. This is a mistake. Starting anything with you. I'm sorry." Sofia tried to turn away, but she couldn't tear her gaze away from his lips.

*One kiss.*

She levered up on her toes, ignoring the pain that shot through her arches. When their lips met, Nick slid his arms around her, but he let her lead. Her tongue teased gently, and he deepened the kiss, exploring, his hands in her hair.

She could lose herself in him. In the sensations flooding her neglected body and soul. But if she didn't run...

"I'm sorry," she whispered. "Goodbye."

As she crossed the threshold into the club, she turned, then wished she hadn't. Nick watched her, the pain in his eyes burning into her soul.

At the end of the night, Sofia locked up the cash register with shaking hands before heading to her boss's office. "Victor?"

He didn't respond. His back to her, Victor's attention was fixed on the security camera footage from the club. Sofia peered through the crack in the door, praying she wouldn't find herself and Nick together on screen. "Get in here, *сýка*."

Sofia flinched and pushed through the door. "H-here's the register key. I'm going home."

"Not yet, you're not." Victor switched camera feeds, and Sofia's heart leapt into her throat. Out on the street, she and Nick locked lips, and the sight of her in his arms, of the way his entire body curved around her, protecting, claiming, both warmed her heart and left her shaking. "Did you do what you were told?"

"He... He doesn't gamble anymore. I told you. I...I asked him why he came. H-he said to see me."

Victor searched her face, and the last chapter of Sofia's text-book came flooding back to her. *People often use the words "ah" and "um" when they're lying. They repeat sentences multiple times, blink rapidly, stand perfectly still, or look to the left when talking.*

She kept her gaze on Victor, cocked a hip, and raised her brow. "Can I go?"

"No. That kiss is not 'we barely know one another.' You have some influence over him." Victor stood, towering over her as he crossed his arms. "Get him back in here on Saturday night. I'll give you the key to the liquor cabinet. By the end of the night, I want him drunk and upstairs. Understand?"

"Please don't do this." Sofia backed up a step, afraid to run, but terrified what would happen if she stayed. "I...like him."

Victor's lips curved into a smile. "I know all about you, *сука*. How hard you work taking care of your sister. How much you need this job. Do this, or you'll never work as a bartender again. Now go home. Use your night off to think about how you'll get Nicholas Fairhaven back to Bound. Don't disappoint me."

Numb, Sofia nodded as she turned and headed back to the bar for her coat. What the hell was she going to do now?

**Nick**

Nick walked the two miles to Cal's house, needing the crisp, spring air to clear his head. After a brisk knock, Cal's wife welcomed him inside. "Nick! It's good to see you." Hannah enveloped him in a warm hug once she shut the door behind him. "Cal's in his workshop. He's been in there all night. I hope you have something good to tell him."

Nick met Hannah's gaze. His friend's wife looked tired, and her eyes shone until she blinked hard. "What's wrong?"

"This case is keeping him up all hours, and I'm worried. He didn't even want dinner tonight." Hannah tugged at the hem of her sweater, the loose material billowing around her thin frame.

"I'll sort him. Worst case, there's a late meeting down at the First Covenant Church in an hour I'd planned to go to. I'll drag him out with me."

"Thank you." Hannah hugged him again.

Cal's workshop consisted of a small utility room in the basement of his brownstone. "Goddamnit," the cop muttered as he dropped a hammer on his foot and hopped around, cursing under his breath.

"Easy there, mate." Nick scooped up the hammer and set it on the workbench. "What're you working on?"

"Birdhouse."

Raising his brows, Nick poked at the lopsided box on the bench. "I hate to tell you, but most birds have standards."

Cal rubbed the back of his thick neck as he sank down onto a stool. "I shouldn't use tools when I'm this tired. But this damn case is killing me, and I needed the release."

"We should find you a safer hobby. I'm afraid I don't have much news on Bound, though." Nick wandered over to the mini-fridge Cal kept in the corner of the room and withdrew two bottles of sparkling water as he explained what had happened at the club.

Cal nodded as he accepted the bottle. "Dammit. I was hoping you'd have *something*. I'm getting a lot of pressure from the higher-ups to find this kid, and everything in my gut tells me she ran away. Parents." He shook his head. "They never want to believe it. And most times, they're right. But this kid? All the markers. Failing grades, a recent tattoo, drinking..."

Cal guzzled half the bottle down. With his neatly trimmed salt-and-pepper hair and precisely shaven beard, he always reminded Nick of the patriarch of the Fairhaven clan. Or at least what Nick imagined Father would look like, had he lived.

"I know many reputable men and women with tattoos," Nick offered. "Including my brother. And failing grades..." Sofia's tear-stained face hovered behind his eyelids. "Many reasons come to mind."

"Twenty-five years of police work tell me she took off on her own. But then that kidnapping you stopped the other day...Emily Norse? The girl won't talk to us. I've left her four messages."

Dammit if Cal didn't sound a bit like Father as well. Except for the lack of a British accent. Nick ran a hand through his hair. "What's your next move?"

Picking up the hammer and turning it over in his hands, Cal shook his head. "I'll get a warrant for Bound and a couple of the other clubs in the area. If I can get a judge to listen without a single shred of evidence." A misshapen shingle fell off the bird-house, and Cal snorted. "Shit. I really suck at this."

The two sat in companionable silence for a few minutes while Cal methodically disassembled the lopsided box. After the last nail dropped into the garbage can, Cal brushed his hands on his pants. "How's your family doing?"

*You just had to ask.*

Loneliness simmered just under the surface, along with anger and frustration. "Alex has very little to say to me these days. The photos of me from the club the other night have caused him no end of trouble, and Elizabeth..." Nick rose and stalked over to the corner of the bench, rifling through the various drawers in Cal's storage cube until he found the right-sized nails for the birdhouse. "She's dealing with some issues with her parents. That's put Alex in a bad state, and he's not his usual understanding self. My attempts at making amends failed miserably."

God, even Nick hated how hollow his words sounded. In truth, he'd completely failed to get through to Alex, though at least his brother had emailed him that evening to tell him the board wasn't calling for Nick's head—at the moment.

Cal laid a hand on Nick's shoulder. "Fair enough. Have you made any progress towards a hobby? Or perhaps a new career?" He brushed splinters from the workbench and raised his brows.

"I have plenty to keep me entertained."

"Oh?" With a sly grin, Cal leaned forward. "You seeing someone?"

Nick bristled at the question. From the look in Sofia's eyes when she'd run from him, she wouldn't call. Even if she did manage to read the note he'd left on his card. "No. However, I spend ten hours a week at the Food Bank on Houston Street."

Cal snorted. "And what the hell do you do with the rest of your time? For fuck's sake, man, I spend more than ten hours a week commuting. You can't tell me that's enough to keep you out of trouble."

Clenching his free hand, Nick counted to five. "For now, yes. I haven't missed a meeting in months, mate. I work out every day, I've learned how to cook, and I enjoy reading. I have feelers out with a handful of charitable organizations, and until one of them returns my calls, that's enough."

*It has to be.*

"Nick, for five months, we talked every damn day. Went to meetings together three times a week. I know you better than you know yourself, son. And I'm telling you, if you don't figure out some sort of purpose in this life, you're going to find yourself falling so fast the bottom won't know what hit it." With a sigh, Cal picked up the remains of the birdhouse, turned it over in his hands, and snorted. "I'm a shit carpenter. I admit it. Burning the hell out of my hand a few years ago fucked with my dexterity. It's a miracle I can still shoot straight. But tinkering around in here makes me happy. You need to stop lying to yourself. Before you lose sight of the truth forever."

The lump in Nick's throat made it hard to breathe. He sucked down a few sips of water before he tried to speak, and when he did, his words came out hoarse and faint. "Fine. I'm bored out of my fucking mind. Not a single charity I've contacted wants anything to do with a recovering gambler who made news for his involvement with the Italian mob.

"I met this intriguing woman—Bound's bartender for fuck's sake—and even had coffee with her this morning. But when I went to the club tonight, she told me she didn't want to see me anymore. At least she warned me about the paparazzi running amok inside. What do you expect me to do? Beg? I volunteer wherever I can, and I spend the rest of my days trying to distract myself so I don't wallow in the life I lost."

Cal reached over and squeezed Nick's bicep. "That's what I wanted to hear, son. Honesty. Look, I'm living proof you can come back from the bowels of hell. I almost lost everything, but despite this fucking case, I'm happier than I've ever been. You'll get there too. As long as you're honest with yourself."

Nick scrubbed his hands over his face. "You're right," he said quietly.

"Now, let's see if we can put our heads together and figure out a plan. We'll get you in with a charity somewhere. The word of a BPD lieutenant ought to be good enough to at least get you an interview."

"While we do that, let me fix this pitiful excuse for a bird-house. I'd prefer not to be shat on next time I come over for dinner." Picking up the hammer, Nick grinned. "You might not believe me, but I know a thing or two about carpentry."

At midnight, Nick paced his living room as a cup of tea cooled on the coffee table. After replaying his meeting with Sofia over and over again in his head, he worried he'd missed something. That she'd lied to him about the paparazzi. But why else would she warn him away? Did she know something about the trafficking ring? Was her boss involved? He kicked himself for leaving her there. The alpha-male protective side of him had wanted to pick her up, carry her to his car, and get her somewhere safe, neutral—somewhere they could talk. The caveman side of him wanted to fuck her senseless. Deep down, though, his heart won the battle with his cock. She wanted space, and he'd give it to her. For tonight, at least. Tomorrow...he made no promises. After Lia...he'd given her space for months and look at where that had landed him. He wouldn't make that mistake again.

Sofia's kiss did him in. He wanted her. Naked. Bound. Begging. But more than that, he wanted to know her. To take her out for dinner, to laugh, and hear her stories. To tell her his. For the first time since Lia, Nick wanted a relationship.

After trying a sip of his now-lukewarm tea, Nick dumped the mug in the sink. He changed into a pair of gym shorts and unfurled his yoga mat. Meditation would help. Or...he'd spend the entire time lost in the memories of that one, passionate kiss.

# 9

## Sofia

SOFIA JERKED awake when something crashed in Gina's bedroom. Her sister's muffled curse followed, and with a groan, Sofia rolled over and shoved her pillow over her head. All their lives, Gina had been the morning person, while Sofia had—by necessity—been the night owl. When the banging continued, Sofia peeked out from under her protective cocoon. Not even 9:00 a.m. and Gina couldn't manage to be quiet?

Trudging towards the bathroom, Sofia stumbled over a large box filled with discarded clothing. Unable to right herself, she slammed into the wall, overcorrected, and missed cracking her head on the kitchen counter by two inches.

"Dammit, Gina. You have a whole bedroom. You can't sort your stuff in there?" Sofia rubbed her aching shoulder as she gingerly pushed to her feet. "You could have killed me."

"I'm almost done," Gina muttered through a crack in her door. She murmured something unintelligible to someone behind her—probably Rick the dick again. A pang of guilt sliced through Sofia's heart. A little over a week and her sister would be gone. A hint of jealousy followed.

"Do you need any help?"

Her sister turned and called, "I've got this," as the door shut.

*Of course you do.*

For the past ten years, Sofia had given up her hopes and dreams so Gina could succeed. No vacations, no splurges, no beauty treatments...all to put her sister through school. And now, Gina was about to backpack across Switzerland before starting her graduate degree in Germany. All on her own. Leaving Sofia with a blackmailing boss who could ensure she had no job—and no options—if she didn't do what he wanted. How many therapy offices would take a chance on her once they saw a police record? None.

Sofia flicked on the coffee pot, and the comforting *whirr* of the grinder, followed by the *glug-glug-glug* of the life-giving liquid promised to fortify her for the day. She'd figure a way out of this.

With a sigh, Sofia leaned a hip against the counter while she waited, listening to the moans and gasps of her kid sister getting frisky with a guy Sofia still hadn't technically met. Sofia had walked Gina to school, helped her through numerous break-ups, tutored her for the SATs, and had driven her to the dorms the very first day of college. Now, it was time for Gina to spread her wings.

Glancing at her mother's statue of the Virgin Mary that watched over them from the top of the fridge, Sofia whispered a quick prayer. "Please keep her safe. And maybe one day, let her come back to me."

Coffee in hand, she retreated to the bathroom for a shower.

Once the sounds of passion from Gina's room stopped, Sofia put down her book. *Principles of Psychoanalysis* had threatened to lull her back to sleep, but she'd powered through two chapters and kicked herself a half a dozen times for her performance on her exam. While she hadn't failed completely, she needed to ace the final if she wanted to graduate. All the answers were there if she'd only managed to study a little more.

"Going out!" Gina yelled seconds before she and *Rick* shot through the door and slammed it behind them.

"Be careful," Sofia murmured, knowing her sister couldn't hear her. "I love you, baby girl."

Now that the apartment didn't feel so much like a war zone, Sofia pulled out her laptop. She had to quit Bound, and her only chance was to find another job first—and pray any background check would go through before Victor and his friends made good on their threats. She marked half a dozen bars in the South End to visit, then remembered a couple of weeks back, she'd picked up a card at an upscale restaurant while running errands. She dug into her coat pocket and found it—along with Nick's business card.

"Why did I have to meet him now?" she asked the plain, unadorned walls of her apartment. "Why couldn't I have finished my undergrad, then run into him at a Dunkin' Donuts or something?"

He'd scratched out his former title—CEO, Fairhaven Exports—and had instead written "Between Careers" under his name. She fought against the smile that tugged at her lips. As she flipped the card over, her cheeks caught fire.

*Have dinner with me? I don't bite, Sofia. Unless you want me to.*

A little thrill shot to her core, and under her baggy sweatshirt, her nipples pebbled. Nick's disarming sense of humor—along with the sadness that lingered in his gaze—called to her. Perhaps her injured soul recognized a kindred spirit. And that kiss.

The bitter taste of regret coated her tongue, and she tried to wash it down with more coffee, but her stomach soured, and she collapsed against the couch cushions, clutching the card to her chest. "I'm sorry, Nick."

By noon, she'd applied for half a dozen jobs online and had appointments at another six bars that evening. One of her rare nights off—with the apartment all to herself—and what was she going to do? Spend it trying to make sure all of her nights for the next ten years were spoken for.

The pounding on her door startled her enough to drop her phone, sending it clattering under the couch. "Damnit." As she dropped to her knees, she called, "Just a minute."

Next to her phone, amid a few sparse dust bunnies, she found a small baggie—empty save for a white, powdery residue.

*Fuck. Gina, what the hell did you do?*

Another knock and Sofia swore under her breath. "You're going to have to wait."

Once she'd flushed the baggie and washed her hands, she was too flustered to bother checking the peephole before flinging the door wide open. "Oh shit."

"That's not the response I'd hoped for," Nick said as he offered her a to-go cup from Artist's Grind. "Especially when I brought a peace offering. Cappuccino?"

"How did you know—?"

"Which apartment? Your name is on the mailbox downstairs." He lifted a brow, nodding at the coffee cup. "I've already had two espressos this morning trying to work up the courage to knock on your door. Any more coffee and I'll start vibrating."

Sofia accepted the cappuccino, cursing inwardly when their fingers brushed and warmth spread up her arm. "Thank you."

Shoulders slumped in defeat, she headed for the living room with her coffee cupped protectively in her hands. He wasn't the type of man to give up if she closed the door in his face. Not that she wanted to.

"Can we talk about last night?" Nick asked as he removed his camel-colored trench coat, folding it carefully over the back of a chair. "*Were* there reporters inside the club? Or is there something else going on?"

Sofia went to the window, staring out over an alleyway— not the best of views, but she needed something to distract herself from the man behind her. "I lied about the reporters," she said softly. "But please trust me. I didn't have a choice."

Nick smoothed his hands down her arms, and she fought not to lean into him. "Talk to me, love."

Unable to muster more than a whisper, Sofia let her head fall back, relishing Nick's scent and the way she felt held in his strong embrace. "I can't."

"You mean you won't." His lips brushed her ear. "I haven't gagged you. Haven't tied you up. Yet."

She flushed. "I wish I'd met you...some other time."

"Why?" Nick rested his chin atop her head. Sofia never wanted to move again.

Unable to think with his scent all around her, she extricated herself from his embrace and skirted the kitchen counter. "I like talking to you," she blurted out. "And, your note..."

"What about my note?" Amusement lightened his words, but under the mirth, the Dominant in him lingered as he pinned her with his icy blue stare.

"It's been years." Her voice cracked, but once her confession tumbled out, the words kept coming. "I haven't dated anyone in so long, and when I saw you at the club the other night, there was something different about you. Not like the other men who come in there every day. You...talked to me. Most of my customers either try to see down my corset or simply bark drink orders at me."

*Stop. You're making a fool of yourself in front of one of the richest men in Boston. Or at least the most well known.*

"You need to work at a better establishment."

Sofia laughed. "No shit."

"The dinner offer still stands. Even if nothing else happens." Crossing the room, he smiled. "Though I very much want something else to happen."

The memory of his lips on hers, the way he felt pressed against her the previous night, and the care he'd shown her every time they'd been in the same room softened her resolve. She wanted this. Wanted him. But she had to know if she could keep him away from Victor's game. If he were still actively gambling, she'd be setting herself up for heartbreak. "Why did you come to Bound last night?"

With a sigh, Nick shoved his hands into his pockets. "You ran out of the coffee shop before I had a chance to talk to you about your boss. A friend of mine—a police officer—is investigating suspicious activity at some of the clubs in Boston. He's concerned Bound might have a dark side."

"It does." She hadn't meant to tell him. Nor could she take her admission back. "You can't say anything. To anyone. And you can't go back there. Ever. They'll find a way to draw you into…"

"Into what?" Nick kept the counter between them, but pressed his palms to the cheap Formica and leaned closer, frustration churning in his gaze. "I assure you, Sofia. I have never been, nor will I ever be, involved with anyone capable of kidnapping young women. Not even the Italian mob. They are many things, all of them evil, but they do *not* deal in sex trafficking."

"What?" Sofia stumbled back, almost losing her footing as her legs tried to fold under her. Grabbing the fridge handle, she forced some strength into her voice. "Who said anything about sex trafficking?"

Nick's brows furrowed. "Cal—my friend on the force—is investigating a string of disappearances. All young women. Several frequented Bound in the weeks before their disappearance. After I told him about the attempted kidnapping the other night, he asked me to go back to Bound. See if I could find anything...suspicious. What dark side are you speaking of?"

Shock had her heart racing. "Gambling. Victor runs an illegal high-stakes poker game upstairs. He...he's pressuring me to get you to join in."

"Shite, love. Is that all?" Nick skirted the counter and wrapped an arm around Sofia's waist, guiding her back to the living room and sinking with her onto the sofa. "I won't lie to you. There are still days placing a bet is all I think about. Addiction is a vicious master. I tried to give up gambling four times before it stuck. Every time...I thought I'd done it. 'Just stop,' I told myself. Why is it so hard? But I'm broken in some way...and gambling soothed the ache inside.

"I'm an addict. For many years, I couldn't say those words, couldn't admit my failings to anyone—including myself. I can now. I wake up every day with the itch to place a bet. But I also live each day knowing how much I hurt my family. I won't let myself be dragged back into that world."

"That's why I want you to stay away. From Bound...and from me." Sofia's voice cracked, and she kept her gaze fixed on his business card resting on her coffee table.

"Sofia." Nick's tone changed. An edge of authority something deep inside her recognized...and needed. "Look at me."

She couldn't do this. Not today. A tear tumbled down her cheek as she gestured to her textbook. "I've always had the worst possible timing. This one class is all that stands between me and my degree. I have to find a new job. Today. Or Victor's going to expect me to bring you into his poker game. I can't just tell him you're not interested. I tried that and he—he told me if I wanted to keep my job, I had to find a way."

A seething, possessive sound, almost a growl, rumbled in Nick's chest, but Sofia couldn't stop herself now. "And my sister... shit. She's seeing this new guy. 'Having some fun' before she leaves the country. I think he left an empty cocaine baggie under the couch. Gina's never done drugs. Hell, she never even rebelled as a teenager. But the past week...it's like she's trying to see how far and how fast she can fall." Sofia dropped her gaze, sending another tear to join the first. "And then there's you."

Nick reached for her hands, linking their fingers and turning slightly so they faced one another. "I can't do anything about my bloody awful timing. Or your sister's poor choice in men. But I will stay away from Bound if it will keep you safe. As for a new job, I know many of the better restaurant and bar owners in town. I could put in a good word..."

"No." Shaking her head, she almost lost control when Nick tucked a curl behind her ear. "I have to do this on my own. I have a dozen appointments in the South End this afternoon."

"Very well." He cupped her cheek, urging her to meet his gaze. The whiskey-colored flecks in his stormy blue eyes glowed brighter as he smiled. "Will you at least allow me to take you to dinner? We can eat late. Say nine? You'll have plenty of time in the South End, and when you're done, you won't have to worry about cooking."

"I..."

*Can't. Shouldn't. Want to more than anything.*

"What's your favorite cuisine?"

Sofia fought the urge to bury her face in her hands. "Ethiopian."

He chuckled, and his face lit up. "Brilliant. Do you know Asmara's?"

"Um, yes. I eat there all the time." Shock lowered her guard. Her mouth watered at the very thought of one of the chef's specialties.

"Meet me there at nine?" Nick asked.

The hope in his tone almost made her forget about Victor's promise to ruin her. "Okay. But...after that...if I don't show up with a job offer, you have to stay away from me for a while. Please. I don't want Victor to know that we're...friends."

"We'll see about that." Nick pulled her against him and claimed her mouth. When he drew back, leaving her breathless, he groaned. "We might be more than friends, love. But I'll protect you. Whatever it takes. As long as you don't shut me out."

He said goodbye with another searing kiss, and as the door clicked shut, Sofia let herself collapse face first into the couch. What had she done?

# 10

**Nick**

HE HAD to fight the urge to call every bar in the South End and put in a good word for Sofia. Only the mail—and another rejection letter from OneFund, Boston's most iconic charity—reminded him that his name held little more value than mud at present. He'd probably do her more harm than good.

Instead, Nick wandered into his bedroom. At his last place, a rich brownstone with two floors and five bedrooms, he had a dedicated playroom. But when he decided to downsize and leave Fairhaven Exports, he'd sold his home and moved into a two-bedroom condo closer to his favorite spot in Boston, the Old North Church. Something about the building had always called to him, though given that Paul Revere had launched his famous "the British are coming" ride there, Nick wondered every time he stepped inside if he were betraying his native country.

Blast it. He'd gone more than a year—nineteen months to be exact—without gambling or dating, and until Sofia had pushed him away the night before, he'd thought he was doing fine. But the few hours he'd spent convinced she'd never give him the time of day again, plus Cal's words about finding his place in the world, had left him with a lump in his throat that hadn't faded until Sofia had agreed to dinner.

He almost picked up the phone to check on Alex and Elizabeth, but with how raw he felt, that was a risk he couldn't take today.

Rummaging around in his closet, he withdrew two boxes, still secured with packing tape. His pocket knife made quick work of the bindings, and he peered into another world. Another life.

Padded leather cuffs, black with cobalt accents, landed on his neatly made bed. Next, he unrolled the deep blue hemp rope, letting the coils slip through his fingers. Fuck, he'd missed this. A soft ball gag looked a bit worse for wear, so he tossed that in the trash, making a mental note to pick up a new one before dinner. His favorite blindfold—the outside covered in black lace and the inside fashioned with soft eye cups—stirred his cock as he pictured Sofia lying on his bed, trusting him with her pleasure. Various clips and hasps tumbled out as he upended the box.

In the next treasure trove, he found two floggers—one leather and one suede—along with three crops, a vibrator, five different anal plugs of various shapes and sizes, and a thin, leather collar. Deep blue, with a small, easy-release buckle and four o-rings, the damn thing made him groan as his jeans suddenly felt very, very tight.

Nick glanced at his watch. He only had a few hours to prepare this room. Not that he counted on Sofia's willingness to accompany him to bed tonight, or even back to his condo. A Master, though, must always be prepared.

## Sofia

Six bars down, five to go. Sofia turned down Dartmouth Street, having two interviews set up for the next afternoon and one on-the-spot job offer. Too bad the pay wouldn't let her quit Bound and afford school. Though the memory of Nick's kiss and his arms around her left her wondering how much money one truly needed to spend on food and heat.

Pulling out her phone as she sank down on a bench inside Copley Place, she stared at her sister's last message.

*Won't be home tonight. Clubbing with Rick.*

Hooking up with a guy her last week in Boston? Gina had always been flighty—in every part of her life other than her studies. This week, though, she'd taken those tendencies and dialed them up to eleven. With a grimace, Sofia tapped out a reply.

*Worried about you, Sis. Are you staying safe? Nothing extreme, right?*

She stopped short of telling Gina about the baggie. Based on where *Rick* had been sitting the day Sofia had found him on the couch, he could have dropped the empty pouch without Gina even knowing. Still...Gina rarely drank, had never done anything stronger than pot, and that only a couple of times as far as Sofia knew. Other than her first month or two of college, she never stayed out late unless she was at the library.

Her sister's answer didn't reassure her.

*You're not Mom. I missed out on so much busting my ass for this internship. Time to live a little. See you Sunday.*

Sunday? "Shit." They'd have so little time together before Gina flew off to Europe. Anger set Sofia's shoulders in a firm line, and she shoved her phone into her pocket so she wouldn't say anything she'd regret.

The short skirt and stockings did little to keep her warm on this unusually chilly April evening. As the sun dipped below the

horizon, Sofia buttoned up her old coat and headed for bar
number seven.

**Nick**

Ten minutes before nine, Nick slipped through the door of
Asmara's. The hole-in-the-wall Ethiopian restaurant offered a
small menu of Americanized items, but all of the regulars knew
to ask for the long menu, where authenticity ruled.

"Welcome, Mr. Fairhaven." Gelila, one of the owners,
approached Nick with a warm smile. "We have not seen you here
recently. Your usual table?"

"I've not had much occasion to eat out lately." Nick bowed
slightly, and when he straightened, Gelila had focused her gaze
behind him. Turning, he struggled for words.

Sofia stood in the doorway, her inky locks tousled from the
spring breeze. That abysmal threadbare coat had fallen open, and
a golden, shimmering blouse clung to her breasts. Before he
could make a fool of himself, Gelila brushed past him. "Sofia!"
The older woman leaned forward and kissed Sofia on both
cheeks. "I didn't see a takeout order for you."

"I'm...um...with..." Sofia gestured to Nick, then shook her
head and stammered, "I'm having dinner with Nick."

Gelila's brows shot up, but to her credit, she said nothing.
She knew of his problems and had even *tsked* him for them
once or twice. Many times she'd suggested he find a nice girl to
settle down with, but he'd always claimed to be an avowed
bachelor.

Unable to form words, Nick twined his fingers with Sofia's,
then brushed a kiss to her cheek. She smelled like white ginger

and in the dim lights of the restaurant, her eyes sparkled. "You look...exquisite."

"I'm a mess," she said, breathless. "I ran from the T station."

"Were you successful?" Though Nick felt Gelila's stare, he had to know. Was this the first and last date they'd have? Or would they have the chance to see where this budding relationship would go?

"Maybe. I won't know until tomorrow." Sofia dropped her gaze to their joined hands. "Can we...not talk about it?"

"For now."

Gelila watched them, amused. "Follow me, you two." With two long menus in her hand, Gelila shuffled off to a quiet corner of the restaurant as Nick and Sofia followed. "I will bring you wine," she said once she'd placed the menus on the table.

Nick helped Sofia with her coat and tried valiantly not to stare at her ass as she slid into the small, corner booth. Her slim black skirt ended at mid-thigh, and sheer stockings disappeared into a pair of tall, black boots.

"Would you prefer beer? Or tea?" Shedding his coat, he cursed his staid white dress shirt, open at the neck, and black slacks. He'd never been particularly stylish, but next to Sofia, he resembled a banker. As he took his seat, their knees almost touching, she shook her head.

"No." Her answer came a little too quickly, and she glanced down at her hands clasped in her lap. "I mean...I enjoy wine."

Nick studied her. Discomfort pinched her features, and her entire body trembled as she bounced her leg under the table. If he did nothing else, he'd get her to relax—or at least laugh. "Gelila has never steered me wrong, but do you prefer red or white?"

"Both. You?"

"When I drink, I usually choose red," Nick offered as he poured her a glass of water from the carafe between them.

Sofia fiddled with her napkin. "When you drink?"

Tension creased his brow as he tried to decide how much more to tell her. "I stopped gambling almost two years ago. At the time, I made a number of other changes in my life. I never drank to excess—not exactly. However, as I barreled towards bottom, I found myself having a glass of scotch every night. Sometimes two. Recovery taught me how to deal with my problems without resorting to alcohol. I still enjoy a drink. Don't misunderstand. And when I'm low...well, the night we met, I'm afraid I tied one on rather thoroughly when I got home."

Gelila saved him from continuing by setting an ornate ice bucket next to the table. She popped the cork on a bottle of crisp white wine and poured them each a glass.

"I will take these," she said as she swept the menus off the table. "My Addisu will prepare something special for the two of you."

Before Nick could respond, she rushed back into the kitchen.

Rather than dwell on the awkward moment, he lifted his wine glass. "To a night of interesting conversation with the most beautiful woman in the room."

As Sofia lifted her glass to meet his, her lower lip wobbled slightly, and he tried not to let his concern dim his smile.

Once they'd each had a sip of wine, Nick leaned closer. "Sofia, what's your safeword?"

---

## 11

### Sofia

"Um...what?" Surprise sent Sofia's heart fluttering, but underneath, a current of excitement electrified her skin. She hunched her shoulders as her nipples tightened and she cursed her choice of the thin, lacy bra.

Nick smiled, the restaurant lights making his blue eyes sparkle. "Your safeword." He reached for her hand and covered her chilled fingers with his. "Relax. I'm not suggesting we play. Yet."

He kept his voice gentle, but the heat of his words belied his tone. "We've danced around this since we met. I believe our interests...in the bedroom...align. I thought you might feel more comfortable if we established your limits now. In case we end this night in bed. Or at least...with you tied to it. Do you have a certain word you prefer? Or do you use green, yellow, and red?"

He rubbed his thumb over the inside of her wrist, the same calming gesture he'd used in the coffee shop, and Sofia took a steadying breath. She wanted this. Gina wasn't the only one who'd missed out on fun all these years. Now, pursued by a hot,

British billionaire—or former billionaire anyway—Sofia didn't want to return to her all-work-and-no-play existence.

"Red." Biting her lip, she forced herself to meet his gaze. "The last time I...played...my safeword was red."

Nick brought her hand to his lips and brushed a kiss over her knuckles. "Thank you, Sofia."

Confusion furrowed her brow. "What for?"

"For trusting me." Nick glanced at her hand resting on his knee. "I haven't wanted to...know anyone in a long time. I'm not looking for a one-night-stand. Or even someone to play with on occasion. Despite what the press might have led you to believe, I'm not that kind of man."

*Oh.* Deep down, she'd known that about him from the first night they'd met. A sadness had lingered in Nick's eyes, probably in part due to his lost love. And though he had flirted shamelessly, a serious tone laced every word. Meeting his gaze now, Sofia could find no trace of discontentment.

She pressed her lips together, hoping to stop herself from blurting out something truly stupid like how she shouldn't be here or how she wasn't the type of woman he should be having dinner with. There was nothing wrong with her. No reason for her to feel inferior, less than worthy, even though somewhere deep down, those thoughts lingered.

"Sofia?" Nick squeezed her hand. "You disappeared. Where did you go?"

"Inside my own head." She sighed, raking her fingers through her unruly hair. "I haven't had a night off—a night out—in...well, years. And I want to know you too. Outside...and inside the bedroom."

Nick's smile warmed her, and they toasted to the evening. After Nick dabbed his lips with a napkin, he cocked his head. "Tell me about your job search. Everything."

"There's not a lot to tell," she admitted. "One of the sports bars close to the waterfront offered me a job on the spot, but they don't pay a cent over minimum wage, and I didn't see enough patrons in there to make up for the difference in tips. But I have two interviews tomorrow, and the bar manager at Spago actually seemed interested. He said he'd call me in the morning."

Nick sat back, respect brightening his features. "That's wonderful. I...I'll offer again. Can I put in a good word anywhere? Or perhaps ask Alex to do so? His recommendation probably carries more weight these days than mine."

"No. I want to do this on my own." Sofia narrowed her gaze at the man across from her. "Promise me. No interfering."

"On my life." He placed his palm over his heart. "That's not who I am anymore."

"Anymore?"

An amused smile curved his lips. "My brother and I grew up privileged. Very. Our father was a shrewd businessman, and our mother has a brilliant head for finances. When you run billion-dollar corporations, you often forget that real people are involved. Fairhaven Exports is the largest shipping company in the world. Negotiating contracts...well, before my *fall from grace*, I'd march into a business meeting and more or less walk all over everyone else in the room. The job required it—or I thought it did. In truth, I simply wasn't the best of men."

Nick had been nothing but caring the entire time she'd known him. Hearing him describe himself in those terms didn't ring true. "And now?"

"Now, I've learned the value of listening. If you change your mind, you have only to ask. I may not have the power of my former position or the resources I once did, but my name is still well known and in a few places, not quite mud. I'd help you in an instant. If you wanted me to."

"Thank you. That you'd offer means a lot. Even if I can't let you." Sofia washed down the tinge of regret that lingered with a sip of wine.

"How long have you worked at Bound?" Nick asked.

"Three years. Victor hired me not long after they opened. I impressed him with my non-alcoholic recipes. Though I also think he knew I was desperate. The pay sucked until I worked up the courage to ask for a raise. It's still not great, but the tips more than make up for the lousy hourly rate. Still, he keeps my hours right under forty a week. Most places around here don't hire full-time employees so they can get out of paying for benefits. Though, as of next week, I won't have to worry about keeping a policy for my sister anymore." She fiddled with her napkin, the intensity of Nick's gaze making her want to squirm in her seat. But that would just remind her of the kiss they'd shared—and how she hoped he couldn't see how aroused she was by his presence.

"How long have you taken care of her?"

A pang of sadness twisted in Sofia's chest. "When I was seventeen, our parents were killed in a car accident. Gina was twelve. The only other family we had—our great Aunt Rita—lived in Florida and couldn't take us in. But she knew a really good lawyer. He had the courts declare me an adult and give me provisional custody of Gina. There were social workers and counselors and all sorts of people involved, but I worked my ass off to make sure that Gina and I could stay together. She's brilliant. Loves science. When she got accepted to Boston College on a partial scholarship, I promised her I'd do everything I could to make sure she graduated with as little debt as possible. She never had to work a day. Graduated top of her class, and now she's got this fancy job..."

*And I'm stuck here slinging drinks and being blackmailed. How could I put my entire life on hold for so long?*

Gelila interrupted Sofia's momentary reverie with a bowl of warm water and two steaming towels on a tray. "Is the wine not good?" she asked, concern lacing her tone.

"It's lovely, my dear," Nick said. "Sofia and I are simply getting to know one another."

Thankful for the distraction, Sofia tried not to blush as Nick took her hands, dipped each in the bowl in turn, and then gently blotted the water away with the steaming towel. She tried to return the favor, but he cleansed his own hands too quickly, his eyes unfocused until Gelila whisked the bowl away.

"I usually get takeout," Sofia said. "I forgot about the ritual."

Nick blinked once, a little longer than usual, and then smiled at her. "As did I."

Before Sofia could ask why he'd stopped visiting a restaurant he so obviously loved, Gelila returned with large dishes filled with injera and several types of wat—a thick stew.

With a smile, Nick raised his wine glass. "Shall we?"

A soft clink punctuated Sofia's reply. "Absolutely."

**Nick**

As Sofia swept up the last bit of stew with a piece of flatbread, Nick marveled at the turn the night had taken. At first shy and hesitant, she now laughed freely at his ridiculous jokes. They shared tales of childhood. He listened raptly when she recounted what she remembered of immigrating to the United States at five and how she'd tried to preserve at least a little of her family's Brazilian heritage for Gina. They chuckled while comparing their citizenship classes, as both held dual passports, and now, they moved on to workplace antics.

"The worst place I ever worked was this bar down in Copley Square," she said after she dabbed her lips with a napkin.

Nick raised a brow, though all he really wanted to do was pull her into his arms and kiss her.

"I know. You'd think such a ritzy area would be a dream,

right?" With a shake of her head, Sofia huffed. "The owner cut all sorts of corners, filling the top shelf bottles with well liquor, buying lemons and limes that were better suited for compost than anything else..."

"Which bar, so I know never to go there again?" Nick draped his arm across the back of the booth, and to his delight, Sofia relaxed against the cushion, her wavy locks tickling his hand.

"Matties." She rolled her eyes. "But don't worry. They were shut down by the health department two years ago. My last day there, I pulled a bottle of eighteen-year-old scotch from the top shelf. The customer was celebrating a big promotion or something—six of his buddies huddled around him. I poured them all doubles, but this was expensive Highland whiskey, and it stank like an ashtray. Turns out, the owner had refilled the bottle with the cheapest Kentucky bourbon he could find, then he'd added a couple of drops of *liquid smoke* to the bottle. Like that smells anything like peat."

"Shite. And he never got caught?" Twining his fingers around a thick curl, he relished the way she turned ever so slightly towards him.

"I'm not sure. I told the customer the bottle was cracked and he'd have to pick another drink. At the end of my shift, I took the 'whiskey' into the owner's office, confronted him, and then quit on the spot." Her eyes darkened, the sparkle fading. "I guess that makes two jobs that have turned ugly on me."

Taking a chance, Nick grazed the back of her neck with his fingers. She leaned into him, and he bent his head so his lips were close to her ear. "Never be sad about sticking up for your principles, Sofia. You're a brave woman."

"Brave doesn't pay the rent." She shook her head, straightened, and when she met his gaze, her eyes were once again clear and almost bright. "Will you excuse me for a minute?"

Nick helped her up, but before she could slip away, he splayed his hand against the small of her back. "Please tell me you're not about to beg off for the night."

His heartbeat thundered in his ears as she brought her hand to his chest. "Not quite yet. There's still dessert." Her eyelids fluttered as she pressed closer, but in the next breath, she turned and headed for the ladies' room.

*Shite. If she doesn't let me kiss her again soon, I might very well implode.* He couldn't tear his gaze from the sway of her hips until she disappeared down the hall. Without her wit and beauty distracting him, he scanned the restaurant as he sank back into the booth. A handful of tables held happy diners, but he'd not seen a dinner rush. He made a mental note to start coming back frequently—and recommending Asmara's to everyone he knew.

He bent to withdraw his phone from his jacket pocket, and a man in a colorful stripped shirt moved in his periphery. Something about his build stuck in Nick's mind, and he leaned forward to see around a pillar.

*No.*

Not Mario Ricci. Not here. Losing his grip on his phone, he rose on unsteady legs. The hunk of plastic and glass clattered to the floor, but Nick didn't care. He had eyes only for the big Italian. Though he felt anything but confident, he strode towards the mobster, only to have the man rise, throw fifty dollars on the table, and practically sprint out of the restaurant.

*What the fuck?* Sparing their still-empty booth a quick glance, Nick pushed through the door, spilling out onto the street with his heart in his throat. A flash of color caught his eye to the left. He surged forward, desperate to catch the man and ask him what the hell he was doing. But a crowd emerged from another local bar, and Nick skidded to a stop, his expensive dress shoes sliding on the damp pavement.

He owed the Italians nothing. Alex had paid his debt without a second thought, his only condition that Nick get help for his gambling problem. So why was Mario following him? If the man had been dining at Asmara's randomly, he'd have simply ignored Nick. To run...

Sofia. He'd left her—and his phone and jacket. She'd be back by now unless her ladies' room excuse had been an escape plan. Despite how ridiculous that possibility sounded to his rational mind, seeing the mobster had shaken him more than he wanted to admit.

*Get a grip.* One of his favorite American sayings, the words— along with his clenched fists—helped him focus. *Get back to the table and beg Sofia's forgiveness.*

As he slipped back inside Asmara's, Gelila frowned at him. "Mr. Fairhaven, I never took you for a rude man."

"I-I'm sorry, Gelila. Please tell me Sofia didn't leave." He tried to peer around the pillar but was stopped by a hand to his chest.

"Sofia has come here twice a month for three years. Takeout, always. Never with a man, never with a friend. Every time with this deep sadness in her eyes and bone weary. Tonight, she is happy. Or was." Gelila lowered her voice. "So were you."

Unable to stop his shoulders from slumping, Nick covered Gelila's hand with his chilled fingers. "You're very observant."

"I am a mother." She held his gaze for another moment before pulling away. "Go. I bring dessert."

When Nick approached the table, Sofia straightened in her seat and held out his phone. "You dropped this."

"Thank you." Their fingers brushed, and the confusion and concern etched on her face made him kick himself even harder. "I thought...a former business associate...we parted on less than agreeable terms."

*Stop. You're making your cock-up worse.* Nick dropped his phone into his jacket pocket without so much as a glance at the screen and then gestured to the booth. "Will you forgive me for running off? It was rude, and I have no excuse other than my brain taking leave of my body."

Sofia nodded, though she kept her distance, pressed against the back of the booth. "Who was he?"

He scrambled for the right words, mesmerized by how her voice shifted with her mood. All night he'd struggled with how much to tell her about his past, only to have their conversation skip over most of the landmines without effort. "As it turns out, he was no one I knew. He just bore a strong resemblance to the gentleman."

Nick laid his hand palm up on the table, hoping she'd take the invitation. Sofia chewed on her lip, a gentle line forming between her brows. As she placed her hand in his, the furrow deepened. "What are we doing?" she whispered.

"Starting something." He cupped her cheek with his free hand and tried not to let his relief show when she smiled. Her sweet scent enveloped him. As their lips met, Sofia's grip tightened.

Shite. She tasted of the wine they'd shared, and her full lips parted when he took the kiss deeper. Tangling his hand in her hair, he held her against him, gently tugging on her lower lip with his teeth until she moaned softly. A single dart of his tongue gifted him with her fingers digging into his hip, and his cock stiffened to the point of pain.

"Sofia," he groaned when he came up for air. "You don't know what you do to me."

She dropped her gaze to his lap and her lips twitched in what might have been a smile. "Oh, I think I do."

After they'd shared dessert—a spicy bread pudding made with injera—Nick held out Sofia's coat and smoothed the wool down her arms. "I don't suppose you'd consider a nightcap...at my flat?"

Sofia turned, her eyes clouded. "I shouldn't."

"Why not, love?" He slid his hand up her back, tangling his fingers in her hair.

"I...don't know." With her body pressed against his, Sofia

chewed on her lower lip until Nick had to brush his thumb over the tortured flesh. "I want..."

"What do you want?" He claimed her mouth, and she slid her arms around his waist. He knew what *he* wanted. Sofia. In his bed. Fear dimmed his arousal a notch as he realized he wanted a lot more than that.

Breathless, Sofia broke off the kiss but didn't pull away. "I want...you."

Nick forced himself to arrest his wide smile so he could slip into his Master persona. "You remember your safeword?"

"Red."

With a nod, Nick tucked her hand in the crook of his elbow. "Good. Shall we?"

# 12

## Sofia

SOFIA HELD onto Nick's arm as he unlocked the door to his Audi A5. A thrill raced through her when he cupped the back of her neck and brushed a kiss to her lips. The scrap of lace under her dress wouldn't do her much good if he kept kissing her, but she didn't want to pull away.

Too soon, Nick drew back, his blue eyes smoldering, streaks of whiskey and aquamarine only increasing his allure. "I don't know that I'll ever get enough of your lips," he said. "I may be a lost cause after I taste the rest of you."

*What are you doing?*

*Living a little—with an incredibly hot guy who's into you. And one you might not be able to see after tonight.*

*Great. Now you're arguing with yourself. Get over it.*

Sofia tried not to let her worries show as he opened her door. Once Nick started the car, he turned to her. "You haven't said a word since we left the restaurant. Are you sure about this?" Concern drew his brows together, and she pursed her lips as he held her gaze. "I haven't had an evening this engaging in years. I don't want it to end. But I'll take you home if you're having second thoughts."

"I'm not...exactly." Sofia reached for his hand as his face fell. "I'm not ready to go home. All day, I kept telling myself this was it. We'd have a nice dinner, and then you'd bring me home. I'd end the night breaking it off with you so I could go back to Bound and tell Victor we weren't involved. And you'd forget about me. I'd be content with the memory of your kiss, with getting to know someone interesting and different and...real. That would be it. Because I wouldn't feel...anything for you."

"And? Do you? Feel something?" Nick tightened his fingers on hers, holding his breath.

"Yes." With a small smile, she looked down at their joined hands. "You know that voice everyone has in their head? The one that's supposed to keep them from doing something they regret?"

He released his breath in a chuckle. "Mine tends to spend quite a lot of time on holiday."

"Mine works *too* well. And it's been arguing with me since my boss told me to drag you into the poker game. I should protect you, I should keep my distance so Victor doesn't try to pressure me again, I should go home and study, I should apply for more jobs, I should find something 'responsible' to do." She shook her head then huffed. "I've had a good time tonight. I like you. We're two consenting adults. Why shouldn't we see where this goes?"

"You sound surprised."

Warm air swirled around them, carrying Nick's scent to her nose. "Wouldn't you be if Boston's cockiest playboy asked you out on a date?"

"I don't swing that way, so...yes, I would be quite surprised. Though I'm not sure who Boston's cockiest playboy is supposed to be these days. Certainly not me. Not after losing"—Nick sighed —"everything."

Sadness lingered in his tone. In the next breath, though, determination returned. "I don't need protecting, love. Not from your boss. I own my addiction, and ultimately, I'm the only one who can protect myself from relapsing. That ass you work for won't send me back down that hole."

"Stay away from Bound. Please. Promise me that." He might not think he needed protecting, but he didn't know Victor. Or the other poker players.

"I told Cal I'd look around. See if I could find any information about the missing women. But I can make inquiries without setting foot in the club. For now." Nick brought her hand to his lips. "We'll figure this out, love. That's one promise I can make. Will you trust me?"

With a shaky smile, Sofia nodded. "I trust you."

**Nick**

Ghosts from Nick's past haunted him the entire drive. His wrist ached where Mario had snapped the bone a few weeks before Nick had entered recovery. The look on Mario's face as he had fled the restaurant had been eerily similar to that night, and Nick feared Forlano had some interest in him again. If so…he was more of a danger to Sofia than she was to him.

He gripped the steering wheel tightly, simultaneously aroused and terrified. The last time he'd found a woman he wanted to *know*—one with wit and poise and determination— he'd lost her because he wasn't brave enough to see what was right in front of him. Now, life had given him a second chance, but fear lingered in Sofia's warm brown eyes. He'd bet what was left of his fortune—he cursed himself for thinking in those terms —she hadn't told him the full story of her boss's depravity.

Winding through the streets of Boston, he stole glances at

Sofia whenever he could. She stared out the window, a look of peace on her face when they sped along the harbor. "I've always loved the water," she said quietly. "When my parents moved us from New Jersey to Boston a year before they died, we used to come down to the waterfront every other weekend. I think Gina and I lived at the aquarium that summer. Gina used to watch the Duck Boats drive out of the water like they were magic."

"At the risk of being too forward, will you have dinner with me again in a few days?" Nick eased the Audi into a parking spot at the end of his block. "There's somewhere I'd very much like to bring you."

Sofia smiled as he reached over to tuck an errant curl behind her ear. "I...I have to find a job. And bartending..."

"Lunch then." He wasn't proud of the desperation in his tone.

"Why don't we start with breakfast tomorrow," she said, her voice taking on a rough edge. "And go from there."

They barely made it through the front door before Nick sunk his hands into Sofia's hair and claimed her mouth. She moaned into his kiss, so soft and light he wondered if he imagined the sound.

Stumbling backwards, he led her to the bedroom, leaving a trail of her coat, his jacket, and his shoes. "Light," she managed when the back of his knees hit the bed. "I...need light."

The slight tremor to her voice sobered him. He flipped on the bedside lamp, bathing the room in a warm glow. "Sofia." His commanding tone, the one he only used in the bedroom, focused her shimmering eyes. "What is your safeword?"

"R-red." Her chest heaved, and she blew out a shaky breath. "I'm sorry. It's stupid. Really. But...I hate the dark."

"Sit, love." Nick pulled open a small cabinet door on his nightstand and withdrew a bottle of water. Once he'd unscrewed the cap and sank down onto the bed next to her, he held the bottle to her lips. "Drink. Small sips. We don't have to do anything you don't want to do."

Sofia let him tend to her until her breathing evened, then she eased the bottle from his hand and set it down. "I promise you, I'm fine. Just...embarrassed. The night my parents died...the power went out. Just me and Gina in the apartment together, pitch dark. I was looking for candles when the police knocked on the door. I'm sorry. I don't know why that hit me all of a sudden."

Easing her back against the pillows, Nick searched her face for signs of panic. Only a hint of shame lingered in her eyes, along with the churning arousal he'd seen in the brown depths all night. "Don't be. It was irresponsible of me to ravage you before we'd set ground rules. Tell me what you like. What your hard limits are."

As he spoke, he ran his hands down her thighs, relishing the feel of the silky stockings against his fingertips. Massaging her calves as he continued his exploration, he waited for her to set the boundaries of their play.

"I don't like being blindfolded. I...need to know what's happening." Sofia's tense muscles started to relax under his touch. "But other than that...oh God, that feels so good."

Nick chuckled as he dug his knuckles into the arch of her left foot. "I almost offered you a foot massage that first night at Bound." When Sofia moaned, he switched to the other arch. "But as I'd just been accused of attacking a woman, I thought I should restrain myself."

"Probably a good idea," she murmured as her eyes fluttered closed. "Plus, I would have melted right off the barstool."

"So, no blindfolds. What else?" Nick drank in the sight of her, black hair fanned around her face on his pillow, arms lazing at her sides, a serene smile curving her lips. "I've always been fond of shibari. Done properly, that is. Not like those idiots at the exhibition."

Sofia sucked in a hissing breath, grinding her hips against the mattress when Nick teased his fingers under her skirt and towards the apex of her thighs. "Yes. I...ahh...like to be tied up."

As he teased the edge of her lace panties, the scent of her arousal perfumed the room, and his cock strained against his briefs. Shite, he'd be lucky if he lasted ten minutes with his beautiful sub. After so long without a partner, without anyone he'd been tempted to bed, Sofia had the power to drive him mad with need.

"Sofia." He brought her back to him with a single word. "I need to hear you say the words. I need to know you want me in control of your pleasure." She reached for him, and he gathered her into his arms. "What do you want, Sofia?"

"You."

"What else?" Nick held her gaze. "Tell me."

Her legs shifted, her nipples tightened to hard peaks under the shimmering gold blouse. "I have to be in control every moment of every day. It's the only way I can work as hard as I do, study, take care of Gina...and not go insane. Here...with you...I need to let go. I only have one hard limit. Darkness. I've been... too busy to date for the past few years, but you know where we met. I understand what I'm getting myself into."

Nick tightened his fingers in Sofia's hair. "Then, my dear sub, shall we begin?"

Drinking in her scent, Nick angled Sofia's head and trailed kisses along her jaw. When he reached the tendon on the side of her neck, he bit down, sucking the sensitive flesh against his teeth. She shuddered and wrapped her arms around him. "Nick..."

"Sir," he half-growled as he nibbled on her earlobe. "In the bedroom, you'll call me Sir."

"Yes...Sir. Please...Sir. Let me touch you." The raspy edge to her voice spurred him on, and Nick palmed one of her breasts, finding the peaked nipple, then pinching. Gently at first, then when she arched against his hand, harder. "Hurts...so good."

"You like a little pain, kitten?" He didn't know where the endearment came from, but it suited her. The little mewls she made as his hand traveled lower and teased over the tight black skirt drove him half mad. "Answer me, Sofia."

"Yes, Sir. I need to...ahhh...feel."

"Off with this, then." Tugging at her blouse, Nick pulled away just enough to slip the shimmering fabric over her head. Her half-lidded eyes churned, golden flecks glowing in the lamplight. "Shite, love. You're perfect." Generous breasts heaved in golden lace, a small tattoo of a phoenix peeking out from the right cup. He kissed the flames where the bird erupted into flight. Bronzed skin, soft and supple, under his hands. A small waist, giving way to generous hips. He found the zipper to her skirt. "This too."

Sofia wriggled out of the restrictive material, and Nick groaned when he saw the garters holding up her stockings. "You undo me."

"You're...still dressed, Sir," she said when he danced his fingers over the matching lace that covered her mound. "Will you—"

"Not yet," he told her. "Arms over your head. Hold on to the headboard."

Her obedience, along with the way she stretched up and offered her breasts as a banquet, was enough to make coming in his briefs a real possibility, but he forced a slow, deep breath to try to relax. "Before I bind you, I want to taste you. Will you let me?"

Sofia's eyelids fluttered. "Yes, Sir. I want your mouth on me."

With a quick tug, the panties slid down her hips. "Spread your legs, kitten. Knees up and apart, feet flat on the bed. Are you able to delay your release until I give you permission to come?"

"Maybe." As Nick bit down on her inner thigh, Sofia corrected, "Sir. It's been a very long time. I'll try."

Her toned legs trembled under his hands, and Nick kissed from one knee up to her mound, then back down. As her breathing turned ragged, he swiped his tongue through her folds, relishing in her essence. Sofia's taste sated something inside him he hadn't known was starved.

Parting her lower lips with one hand, he slid a finger inside her slick channel. "Please, Sir," she keened. "I won't...last. Not the first time."

*Neither will I.*

"Let yourself go," he ordered against her as he traced patterns on her clit and slipped another finger inside. Thrusting deeper, he found her G-spot; when he scraped his teeth against her nub, she flew over the edge with a scream.

When the quakes of her release subsided, Nick gently pried her clenched fingers from the headboard. "Kiss me, Sofia."

Draping her arms around his neck, she obliged, her tongue teasing his. When she sucked his lower lip between her teeth, his need to claim, to control, to have her bound and begging swamped him.

"Undress me," he ordered as he got to his feet. Sofia grabbed his arm as she tried to stand, her legs buckling. "Take it easy, love. Do you need a minute?"

"No, Sir." She smiled, though she kept her eyes downcast as her fingers danced over the buttons of his dress shirt. "I'm still green."

Fuck. The shirt slipped from his shoulders, and his cock throbbed when she pressed a kiss to his collarbone. Her lips traveled lower, and she sat on the edge of the bed while she undid his belt, then his pants. When he was down to his briefs, he kicked the pile of clothing aside. "How do you like to be bound, Sofia? Legs? Arms? Both?"

Nick withdrew a long coil of hemp rope from the drawer, tugged the knot free, and looped the strand around her back, tugging gently to urge her to rise so he could trap her against him.

With a trembling breath, she met his gaze. "Whatever pleases you most, Sir. For tonight, I'm yours."

"Then turn around and give me your wrists."

The toned muscles of her back shifted as she presented herself to him. He looped the rope around her wrists, placing the end just out of the reach of her fingers. "Tell me if this is too tight." His lips brushed her ear as he secured the knot and she tested the bindings.

"It's not, Sir." Sofia rocked against him, and he slid his hand around to cup a breast and drag a thumb over her nipple. "More."

With a practiced motion, Nick wound the rope around her arms, crossing the strand over, under, and through the loops. "You are a vision, Sofia," he said as he draped the rope over her shoulder and around a breast. "Submitting to my restraints."

Back to her arms, he wound the rope around above her elbows, then around the other breast. The position left her shoulders thrust back, her nipples hard peaks, and her chest heaving. The braided pattern along her upper arms would leave gentle impressions in her skin for hours, but he checked her circulation, having her wiggle her fingers before he kissed her palms to ensure they were still warm.

"Sir," she whispered. "I..."

Her shudder worried him, and he gently turned her around. "Does anything hurt? I can remove—"

"No, Sir," she said quickly. Sofia kept her eyes downcast, but Nick cupped her chin, urging her to meet his gaze. Her cheeks reddened as she chewed on her lip for a moment. "I've never felt so...secure."

Brushing a tender kiss to her lips, Nick cradled her against him. "Has no one ever bound your arms this way?"

"No. Not like this. I can't move. Not even a little. It's...wonderful."

Her arousal infused his every breath. He suspected if he slid his fingers along her folds, he'd find her dripping. "In the bedroom, I control your pleasure. I won't disappoint you, love. Your needs come first. Always."

Feathering kisses along the ropes crisscrossing her breasts, he lavished attention on each tight nipple before guiding her against the bed, facing away from him.

"Bend over, kitten."

He helped her lower her torso to the bed and rubbed his hands over the round globes of her ass, warming the skin. "I want you begging. This lovely, smooth skin red from my flogger."

Sofia responded by canting her hips to offer him better access. "You'll have to hold me down, Sir. I...move a lot when flogged."

"Oh?" Nick pulled a set of ankle restraints from his drawer. "Then spread your legs." Once he'd secured her legs to the bedposts, he slipped two fingers inside her channel. She keened, her legs trembling. "Count for me."

"One," she said with a gasp as the flogger landed across her right ass cheek. The second strike landed on her left cheek. "Two."

By the fifth strike, her voice started to fail. By the tenth, she was wriggling so much even with how he'd bound her, that he dropped the flogger and shed his briefs. Once he'd rolled a condom over his length, he wrapped his hands around her hips and nudged at her entrance.

"Shite. You're so fucking wet." Nick groaned. "And tight."

Slowly, letting her get used to his length, he admired his gorgeous sub. The deep blue rope against her skin, her hair tumbling over her shoulders, the red stripes he'd left on her ass... he might not ever get enough of her.

With his fingers twined in the ropes that secured her arms, Nick thrust deep, and Sofia cried out. "Harder...Sir!"

He obliged, but it had been too long, and when she pushed back against him, meeting him thrust for thrust, he crested the wave of his release, and Sofia let go with him.

## 13

**Sofia**

BACON. Sofia rolled over, stretching under the luxurious sheets as the scents of breakfast made her stomach growl. She ran a hand over her ass, relishing in the slight burn that remained from the previous night's flogging.

Hours of play, Nick's tender aftercare, and nightcaps of chamomile tea with bourbon and honey had faded into a deep, dreamless sleep.

Sofia shrugged into Nick's shirt and padded down the hall in search of the delicious scent of breakfast. The sight of him at the stove wearing a black apron—and nothing else—sent her heart racing. "You realize you're every woman's fantasy right now?"

With a chuckle, Nick turned, and in morning's gentle light, he looked so much younger than his forty-one years. Tousled blond hair fell over his forehead, and unshaven, his casual smile warmed Sofia down to her bare toes. "I'd planned to bring you breakfast in bed. Getting dressed seemed like too much effort. Until I started frying bacon."

She laughed, leaning against the kitchen counter to peer into the pan. "Good call. No one should risk cooking bacon naked. I rather like your...assets. It would be a shame to see them...damaged."

"My *assets*?" Nick gestured towards the growing bulge under his apron. "You'd like my cock again before the morning's over? Is that what you're saying, kitten?"

"Yes, Sir." The memory of being on her knees, her arms bound behind her, and Nick's hand in her hair as she sucked him dry brought a small shiver. "Or you could try something else..."

With an arch of his brow, Nick pulled her against him. "Who gives the orders in the bedroom?"

"You do, Sir. But you can't blame a girl for asking." She snagged a piece of bacon and tried to wriggle out of his arms. But he slapped her ass gently, and the sting from the still-healing welts flooded her with arousal.

"Would you like to be punished, Sofia? That could be arranged." Nick released her and almost growled as her nipples hardened to points under the white material. "I may never want that shirt back. Now get back in bed so I can pretend to be a gentleman and bring you breakfast before I tie you up again."

"Yes, Sir."

As Sofia reached the bedroom, someone pounded on the front door. Seconds later, Nick cursed from the other room. "Bloody inconvenient timing," he said as he hurried in, dropped the apron on the bed, and snagged his robe from the closet. "Detective Sampson—from the club the other night—is outside. I'm assuming with more questions about the kidnapping. Stay here. I'll put him off. I can go down to the station this afternoon."

"Okay." Sofia pulled the covers up to her waist, debating whether she should get dressed. She hadn't heard from Gina. She snagged her purse from the floor. She'd just pulled out her phone when Nick's angry voice carried down the hall.

"What the fuck do you think you'll find?" he spat. "I saved that young woman. Ask her."

"We can't," a rough voice said. "She disappeared yesterday. Now kindly step aside and let the officers do their job."

*Oh shit.* Sofia scrambled out of bed and pawed through the pile of clothes on the floor, searching for her skirt. Nick's pants, his briefs, socks...there!

"You'll wait right there until I call my lawyer."

"Fine. But I'm going to watch you dial. Is there anyone else here with you?"

Sofia fumbled for her skirt. She'd just tugged the material over her hips when a uniformed officer appeared in the doorway. "Miss? Are you all right?" His hand hovered over his sidearm as he scanned the room, and his lips pressed into a thin line. "Detective? We've got ropes, a gag, and a whip in here." The officer took a step closer to Sofia. "Are you here of your own free will?"

She held the lapels of Nick's shirt closed over her breasts as she backed away. Confusion furrowed her brow. "Of course. Why wouldn't I be? Do you mind? I'd like to get dressed."

"I can't leave you alone, miss," the officer said. "We're executing a search warrant. You could be destroying evidence."

"Of what? For fuck's sake, we had sex. Pretty sure that's not a crime." Sofia turned slightly so she could button the shirt higher and zip up her skirt.

The officer didn't answer right away, but when Sofia glanced over her shoulder, the vague discomfort on the guy's face worried her. His fingers twitched. "Nicholas Fairhaven is a—"

Nick ducked around the officer. "Sofia?" He held out his hand, the strain in his voice lending a hoarse tone to his words. "Come here, love. We need to wait in the living room."

"What's going on?" Sofia whispered as Nick's arm tightened around her.

He practically vibrated with anger as he led her to the loveseat. When they sat, he brushed his lips against her ear. "My lawyer's on his way. Until Ben gets here, don't answer any questions. This has to be some sort of mistake."

"This is related to what happened at Bound the other night?" Sofia clasped Nick's hand tightly. Other than the night of her parents' death, she'd never had to deal with the police before the attempted kidnapping. Never had a speeding ticket, never been a victim of any crime. But the officer...

*Did they think Nick kidnapped her?*

"Yes." Nick pressed his cheek to hers. "The girl disappeared. They seem to think I had something to do with it. I don't know what evidence they have. They won't tell me. I need to make a few calls—Alex, my friend Cal—but I won't do that in front of them, nor will I leave my flat while they're here."

"Excuse me." One of the officers loomed over them, holding Sofia's wallet, and she flinched. "I'm Officer Tramway. Are you Sofia Oliviera?"

"Um, yes." Sofia pressed closer to Nick. "Is there some reason you had to go through my purse?"

"I'd like to ask you a few questions." Officer Tramway took a seat in the chair across from them, and Nick stiffened.

"No. She doesn't answer any questions until my lawyer arrives. I don't remember asking you to sit down. Execute your warrant, officer, and then kindly leave. As you can see," he said as he gestured to the kitchen, "we were about to have breakfast."

With a glare, Officer Tramway snapped his notebook shut and stood. "Your lack of cooperation will be noted."

"Wh-what?" Sofia's voice rose, indignation coloring her tone. "Now wait a—"

"Sofia." Nick's eyes churned, his irises darkening as his voice took on the same commanding tone he'd used in the bedroom the previous night. "Wait for Ben. Please."

With a sigh, she tried to relax into his embrace, but she felt so exposed sitting there, barefoot, with Nick's white shirt barely hiding the dark points of her nipples and her skirt riding up her thighs. How could he remain so calm? The police had no reason to suspect him of anything—and hell, he'd been with her all night.

They sat in silence for half an hour, Nick stroking her arm or drawing slow patterns on the back of her neck, Sofia with her hand on his thigh and her head on his shoulder. The officers were messy, pulling down books from his bookshelf in the corner of the room, rifling through his kitchen drawers, not bothering to put anything back.

As Officer Tramway opened a burled wood box on the mantle, Nick let out a ragged breath and gripped her leg hard enough she feared she might end up with a bruise.

"That...is precious to me," he said through clenched teeth. "Kindly be careful."

Holding up a platinum necklace with a heart-shaped diamond pendant and a small vial of liquid, Officer Tramway raised a brow. "What's this?"

"Memories," Nick said as he pushed to his feet. "Those belonged to my" —he clenched his fists at his sides—"Lia. She died many years ago."

"Bag the vial," the other officer said.

Nick's voice cracked. "No. Please. It's...perfume. Just her perfume."

"Only way to be sure is to take it to the lab. You tried to drug the woman the other night."

"Get out of my home," Nick spat. "I don't know who the fuck set you on me, or why, but you'll find nothing that links me to that poor woman because I didn't have anything to do with her disappearance. I didn't drug her. I saved her from being carried out of there unconscious."

A muscle in Nick's jaw throbbed as he faced off with the policemen. Sofia feared he'd end up arrested if he didn't calm down. She rose and rested a hand on his arm. "Nick." Leaning closer, she dropped her voice. "I'm scared. Please sit down."

He met her gaze, but his expression warned her this was about to get ugly.

When the knock came, they both flinched. "Nick? What's going on here?" A tall man, a little over fifty with gray streaks in his brown hair pushed through the door.

Nick blew out a breath. "About bloody time. Officers, my lawyer. Benjamin Hetherington."

**Nick**

An hour later, after the police finished destroying any semblance of order in his home, the officers carried Lia's perfume and collar out in evidence bags.

In truth, he'd actually forgotten about the perfume. For the first time in eight years, the anniversary of Lia's death hadn't sent him into a complete tailspin. The difference? Sofia. She'd stayed by his side the entire morning, offering what comfort she could—even though she was as frightened and unsettled as he was. As soon as the police had finished, she'd started a pot of coffee, and now, she headed for the loveseat with two steaming mugs.

"Are you okay?" She sank down next to him and took a sip, shoulders slumping as she swallowed.

Was he? No. He might never be okay again. Ben had made half a dozen calls without discovering anything more about the source or rationale for the warrant. With all his faults, he'd never raised his hand to another person who wasn't currently attacking him. Hell, the punch he'd thrown at Bound the other night had been his first in more than ten years.

"I don't know. I need to make some calls. See Cal. Give Ben some time to find out what the fuck started all of this. And then I need to see my brother. You can bet your ass the *Babbler* is going to find out about this somehow—if they haven't already. Alex is going to be livid."

Sofia's gaze flitted between Nick and her coffee. "I...um, I hate to ask. But...Lia was the woman you lost eight years ago?"

He'd tried to prepare himself to discuss Lia. After dinner the previous night, he'd known his feelings for Sophia were serious and potentially long-lasting. Something about her calmed the beast inside him, and he wanted her in his life for more than just a single date and long night of passion.

"Yes. They took the last pieces of her I had left."

"I'm so sorry." Sofia rested her hand on his arm, and when he risked raising his head, he found understanding. "That was... smart. Keeping the perfume." Her lips curved into a sad smile. "I used to buy my mom's brand of shampoo. I never used it—*I* didn't want to smell like her—but I'd open the bottle and pour some in a little bowl at night whenever Gina and I would have a fight or when I'd have nightmares. Made me feel like she was there with me, and I'd talk to her."

"I'm not sure most women would be quite as understanding as you are," he said. "Not after the night we shared."

One corner of Sofia's mouth curved as she squeezed his hand. "I'm not most women."

"No. You definitely are not."

"We all have baggage, Nick. People in our past we miss, relationships we'd rather forget about, loves we've lost. She was special. I won't replace her—no matter where this goes—and I'd never want to."

He offered her his hand as he rose. "You are a treasure. I wish we had more time this morning. I'll take you home on my way to meet Cal. We can...at least shower together. I'm sorry they ruined breakfast...and other activities."

Sofia frowned as they reached the bed. "Dammit. The officer came in before I could check my phone." One glance at the screen and her face paled, tiny lines around her eyes tightening as she swallowed hard. "I haven't heard from my sister since yesterday afternoon. It's after eleven. She's never this...flaky. I need to go."

"I'll drive you." He felt like a bloody fool for how much he needed her. But he wasn't the only one with problems. If her sister was in trouble, he wanted to help. "If she's not at your flat, we could—"

"You're due to meet Cal in an hour." Sofia rested her hand on his arm and stared up at him, her eyes weary. "I can take care of myself, Nick. Right now, you need to focus on you. On sorting out this mess. My sister's stupid rebellious streak and the fight we're about to have aren't your problems. I'll be fine. Just...call me when you know anything, okay?"

Nick nodded. As she pulled her boots over her bare feet, he kicked himself for being so selfish. He watched the woman he'd started to fall for pack her stockings and panties in her purse and shrug into her bra. "Keep the shirt," he said. Deftly, he buttoned the white Oxford so it just covered her ass, smoothing the long sleeves down her arms. "It's stupid, really. But I like the idea of you wearing something of mine."

She offered him a sad smile. "I have two interviews this afternoon. If they go well, meet me tonight for dinner. My place. If not...then I'll be at Bound, and you need to stay away. But...know I'll be thinking about you."

Their parting kiss felt more like a final goodbye than "see you later," and Nick couldn't figure out why his heart threatened to crack in two as she walked out the door.

## 14

Nick

THE EIGHTEEN-MONTH CHIP tumbled over his knuckles from index finger to pinky and back again. Alex had taught him that little trick one Christmas when they were teens, and now, Nick stared at the shiny edges of the coin, letting the light calm him.

The coffee shop patrons bustled around him, but the whirr of the coffee grinder, the hiss of the frothing wands, and the chatter faded as the chip's motion lulled him into a meditative state.

"Nick?"

Cal slapped a hand on his shoulder, and the chip tumbled to the floor. "Must be bad," the aging cop said as he stooped with a groan to retrieve the coin.

"You could say that. Can I get you anything?" Nick gestured to the barista, but Cal shook his head as he dropped into a chair. Smudges bruised Cal's eyes, and his normally pink cheeks held little color.

A momentary pang of regret bloomed in Nick's chest, and he swallowed his pride. "I think I'm in trouble, mate. Real trouble."

"You and me both," Cal muttered. "But what can I do?"

"Tell me why two cops showed up at my door this morning with a search warrant."

"Shit." Cal rubbed the back of his neck. "I didn't know, Nick. You've got to believe me. My captain took me off the case." With a small shake of his head, Cal met Nick's gaze. "Because of you."

"Bloody hell. So I'm a suspect, then. This wasn't some...fluke or pressure from the *Beantown Babbler*? For fuck's sake, why?"

"I don't know. I told Sitwell you couldn't have had anything to do with it, but he muttered something about addicts sticking together and dismissed me. I'll be lucky if he doesn't reassign me to desk duty after this."

"They can't have anything on me." Nick's phone buzzed in his jacket pocket, and he held up his hand. "Give me a minute. I have to take this."

Cal inclined his head as Nick headed for the door. Sunlight warmed his cheeks, but Nick still felt a chill as he swiped across the screen. "Alex."

"Have you seen the papers?"

"I'm fine, brother. How are you?" When Alex didn't reply, Nick rolled his eyes. "I haven't, yet. But as the police executed a search warrant this morning, looking for God-knows-what at my flat, I can only imagine. I'm trying to figure out why."

"I'm in Seattle with Elizabeth. We'll be back in two days—I hope. The board is calling for your permanent removal, and at least two of the members have suggested that I resign as well." Alex's voice bore the strain weighing on Nick's shoulders. "Fix this, Nicholas."

"Do you think this is fun for me? For fuck's sake. The woman I'm seeing was with me this morning when the police arrived. I'll be lucky if she answers my calls after this."

"You're...dating?" Shock softened Alex's tone, and he murmured something Nick couldn't hear before returning to the line. "Do you think that's smart?"

Nick's last nerve frayed and he bristled. "You're not Father,

Alex. Yes, I'm seeing someone. She's highly intelligent, a perfect sub, and different from anyone I've ever met. Sound familiar?"

"What's familiar is your name in the papers. Please at least tell me you're staying away from the track."

Nick ended the call. He'd never live down his failures. Not in Alex's eyes. Trudging back inside, he took the seat across from Cal. "My brother believes all this negative press is sending me back to the track."

"And is it?" Cal's hands shook as he spread his fingers out on the table. "You're one of the few people in my life who can understand how much I want a drink right now."

"I have no desire to lose everything. I'm not cured, mate. I'll always have this monster inside me. I miss the rush. The thrill of placing a bet. Lia...the hole she left won't ever fully close. But I've seen bottom. Crawling out of Forlano's office with a broken wrist and driving myself to the hospital? Seeing one of the brute's enforcers with his hands on Elizabeth? I won't go there again. I'll find a meeting every hour of every day rather than fall down that hole again. Last night was the first night in two years I fell asleep without the need burning inside me. I want more of those nights."

*More of Sofia.* Memories of her bound and begging warmed him as Cal sat back in his chair. Damn. Hopefully, this morning hadn't screwed everything up. She hadn't responded to his text, and he wasn't proud of how that disappointment ate at him.

"Listen, Nick. I can't tell you anything—officially. If Sitwell finds out we're talking, he'll probably suspend me. I'm only here because I don't think you had anything to do with the kidnapping and I had to know how you were doing. But the girl—Emily Norse—she couldn't identify the man who attacked her. We sent a sketch artist to the hospital, and she kept getting confused. One minute the guy had blond hair, the next his hair was black. He was tall, he was big, he was thin. The asshole gave her Rohypnol. It messes

with your short-term memory. And now that she's disappeared... rumor is, whoever tried to take her the first time
succeeded."

"What about the club's Masters? They saw the guy." Nick
scrubbed his hands over his face, suddenly worried he could be
in real trouble.

"They say they saw a man run out of the room. And you,
holding an unconscious girl."

"Fuck me."

Cal narrowed his bloodshot eyes and lowered his voice. "Get a
good lawyer, Nick. And be careful."

**Sofia**

Trudging up the stairs to her apartment, Sofia prayed Gina had
made it home all right. Or anywhere. Her usually studious sister
had changed the past few months and Sofia had been too busy to
notice.

The drugs? *Had* they been Gina's?

"Sis?" Sofia called as she pushed through the door.
"You here?"

Only silence greeted her. Nick's words came back to her.
*"Addiction is a vicious master. One taste is all it takes. I tried to stop
gambling four times before it stuck. Every time...I thought I'd done it.
'Just stop,' I told myself. Why is it so hard? Why is it so hard? But I'm
broken in some way...and gambling soothed the ache inside."*

Bypassing the rest of the apartment—and Gina's packing
nightmare—she slipped into Gina's room. "I can't believe I'm
about to do this," she muttered as she opened Gina's top dresser
drawer. A small pile of panties and socks remained. One-by-one,

Sofia unfolded the socks, checking for drugs. Nothing. Sweaters followed. Then yoga pants. Then t-shirts.

Sofia blew out a breath. The closet was also clean. "I guess I can start moving my stuff back in here." She checked her phone again. No messages. "Gina's an adult. She can do what she wants."

Except baby sister was barely twenty-three. Did she really know enough about the world to move to Germany—alone? Or to hook up with a guy she'd just met four days ago? As Sofia headed for the shower, she sent her sister a message.

*I hope you're okay. Miss you. I have a couple of interviews today. If they go well, I can rearrange my plans for tonight and stay home. Popcorn and Casablanca?*

Outside Maldon's, one of the ritziest restaurants in the South End, Sofia smoothed her hands down her black silk shirt. She'd dressed conservatively but had a short skirt in her messenger bag for her next interview—a college bar in Back Bay.

As she took a deep centering breath, someone bumped into her from behind. Her bag fell off her shoulder, spilling her keys and lipstick onto the pavement. "Dammit," she hissed as she glared at the big guy shuffling away. She almost called out to him, but when he turned to glance back at her, her heart stopped. She'd seen him before. Going into Victor's poker game. He hadn't been there the other day, but...he was a regular.

Coincidence. It had to be. No one associated with Bound would know she was here. Unless...Maldon's owner knew Victor. Her phone buzzed.

*My friend's news was not reassuring. My meeting with Ben was delayed until three. I'll call you after that. Good luck with your interviews. -N*

God. She needed Nick right now. A hug. A kiss. Some of his confidence. But if she didn't get inside, she'd blow the interview before she even said hello. She'd respond to him when she was done.

*Where are you?* After her second interview—and the humiliating task of changing into her micro-miniskirt in the bar's tiny bathroom—Sofia texted her sister again. Still without a job offer, she was going to have to go back to Bound tonight. Maldon's promised to give her an answer by Monday, but the bar wouldn't finish their interviews until then.

On her way up her apartment building stairs, she tried to give herself a pep talk. "You'll march up to Victor, tell him Nick is busy, and but he'll be in next week. That gives you seven whole days to find a job. He can't argue with that. Nick will stay away from Bound. He'll do that for me. Everything will be okay."

If only she could pull off the lie. Her mother used to tell her that the truth shone in her eyes like a neon sign. As she closed the apartment door, her phone finally buzzed with a message from Gina.

*Going to Atlantic City for a couple of days. Last big adventure before the big adventure. You'll have to sing along to the movie on your own. Be back on Sunday. Love you.*

Sofia wandered into the kitchen with tears burning in her eyes. Sing along? She never sang along. Not since their mother died. At least she got a *love you*. That was more than her sister had ever said before.

Something crunched under her feet. "Oh my God." The statue of the Virgin Mary from the top of the fridge lay in pieces on the linoleum. As she stooped to clean up the mess, she let her tears spill over.

**Nick**

Ben Hetherington's office overlooked Boston's Inner Harbor. Nick accepted a cup of coffee from Ben's assistant and stared out the window while he waited for his lawyer to finish his previous appointment. Pulling out his phone, he sent Sofia a text.

*I hope you're all right. Please tell me if you're going to Bound tonight.*

He wasn't proud of the death grip he had on his phone. After his meeting with Cal, Nick had returned home to clean up the mess the police left behind. They'd gone through the drawer of sex toys and had taken the hemp rope and the blindfold. At least they'd left the leather cuffs and collar. Wiping the fingerprint dust from the nightstand, his hope for a future with Sofia dimmed. She knew he hadn't had anything to do with Emily Norse's kidnapping, but who wanted to date a man under investigation for such a thing? Her text message did nothing for his mood.

*I have to. I'm going to tell Victor that you had another engagement tonight. Please stay away from Bound. And me. I think he's having me followed.*

Anger flared, along with a deep, possessive need to protect her. Staring at his phone, he tried to come up with a suitable reply that didn't paint him as a caveman. Or a total prick. His first attempt, "Like hell I'll stay away. If he's having you followed, I'm going to park myself at the bar all night," probably wouldn't go over very well.

"Nick? Come on in." Ben held his office door open, and Nick shoved his phone back into his pocket. Probably safer for him to call her after this meeting.

Rich leather chairs, a dark, cherry wood desk, and a small conference table lent an imposing air to the room. "I've made a dozen calls in the past few hours. It's not looking good."

"Fuck. How? I saved a woman's life. Or tried to. The police don't know what happened to her?"

"No." Ben brought up a file on his laptop. "Officially, there's no public statement about Emily Norse. Unofficially...my Boston PD contact says that Emily Norse checked herself out of the hospital the day after the attack. She hung out with her roommate for a few hours, got a couple of calls, but then the roommate left the apartment at 9:00 p.m. When she came back, the place was a mess—like there had been a struggle—and Emily wasn't there. She hasn't been seen since."

Nick cracked his neck, trying to relieve the headache brewing behind his eyes. "Who called her?"

"Unknown numbers."

This day couldn't get much worse. Nick sank back in the chair. "So what do I do?"

"You let me handle shit. Stay away from Bound, don't let the press catch you anywhere but home, the gym, the soup kitchen. For the next few days, Nick, you're a monk. Understand?"

With a nod, Nick thought of Sofia. Monks didn't date. "What about Sofia?"

Ben arched a brow. "She works at Bound. Any association with that place—or with her—is going to work against you. Try to see things from the police's perspective. If you continue to be seen with her while this investigation is going on, they could decide that she's a convenient suspect. Slip a little Rohypnol into a victim's drink, send them into one of the private rooms where you're waiting..."

"That's bloody insane." He shot to his feet, the desire to hit something growing by the minute. "She has nothing to do with this cock-up."

Ben held up his hand. "That doesn't matter. Like it or not, you've got a target on your back. The only way you can get rid of it is to be a fucking saint until the heat dies down."

Nick left Ben's office with a headache and an order to go straight home. Phone in hand, he almost called Sofia, but...what would he say? He'd probably beg her not to go to Bound and come over, and Ben would have his head. Or worse.

Reading her message again, he didn't notice the shadow in his path until he collided with a huge man wearing a long leather coat. "Sorry, mate—"

The apology died in his throat as he came face-to-face with Mario Ricci.

## 15

## Nick

MARIO GRABBED Nick's arm and steered him towards a black town car. "Forlano wants to see you. Now."

"That's not going to work for me," Nick spat and tried to wrench his arm free, but they'd reached the car, and two more of Forlano's men emerged from the front seat.

"If you want to keep that face of yours looking pretty, shut up and get in." Mario opened the back door and shoved Nick onto the seat. "Boss said to bring you in. So that's what we're doing."

Too angry and shocked to think clearly, Nick fumbled with his phone until Mario snatched the device out of his hands. "I'll keep that *safe* for now."

"I don't owe your boss a dime. What the fuck is this all about?" The car pulled away from the curb, and through the tinted rear windows, Nick feared he saw his life streaming by on the busy Boston streets.

No one answered him. After another two futile attempts at questioning Mario, Nick slumped back against the seat. At a stoplight, he considered jumping out of the car, but Mario hadn't taken his eyes off Nick once. He'd be lucky to touch the door handle before the man broke his wrist again.

Half an hour later, they pulled into a back alley in the North End behind Forlano's restaurant—Damian's Trattoria. Another suited thug opened Nick's door and gestured for him to get out of the car. Once the guy—Nick thought his name might be Silvio— patted Nick down, Mario prodded Nick through a dark hallway and shoved him into Forlano's office.

Damian, the head of the Forlano crime family, sat behind his desk with a cup of espresso at his elbow and a fat file folder open in front of him. "I figured if I ever saw you again, Nick, it'd be to loan you another ten grand."

"I don't gamble anymore. Care to explain why your crew felt the need to abduct me off a public street?" Nick balled his hands into fists at his sides, glancing behind him to verify that yes, Mario was once again standing close enough to snap his wrist.

Tossing a black and white photo on the edge of the desk, Damian raised a brow. "Where is she?"

*Emily Norse. Shite.* "Why does everyone think I had something to do with that girl's disappearance?" Nick straightened his shoulders and tried to transfer his weight to the balls of his feet. "I never even spoke to her."

"I had an interesting visitor the other day," Forlano said as he reclined in his chair. "Victor Petrov."

"Why would Bound's owner come to see *you*?" Thoughts swirled in Nick's head, and he wished Mario would let him get away with fishing his chip out of his pocket. He needed to think, to concentrate.

"To ask about you, Nick. Your tells, your predilections, your favorite haunts. How best to lure you in." With a smile, Damian rose and skirted his desk. He grabbed Nick's lapels and hauled him almost off his feet. "My family's been running the gambling scene in this town for more than a century. I don't like anyone honing in on my turf."

"For fuck's sake, Damian. What part of 'I don't gamble anymore' didn't you understand?" Nick crashed into Mario when Forlano released him. The thug shoved Nick against the wall and drove his fist into Nick's side. Trying not to retch as his knees hit the floor, Nick forced himself to breathe through the pain. "What the hell...does this have to do with...that missing girl?" he wheezed as he braced his hand on Forlano's desk and struggled to his feet. "I swear...on my life...I don't know anything about her. I found her in a back room at Victor's club with a guy bigger than Mario trying to shove a needle into her neck. I *saved* her that night."

Damian arched a brow as he studied Nick's face. "You're not lying."

With great effort, Nick managed not to roll his eyes. "I'm an addict. I don't *sell* women. I don't hurt women."

"According to my sources, Victor Petrov does. You've gone to the club on successive nights. I had to be sure you're weren't in his pocket, too."

*Fuck.* Sofia worked for that piece of scum. His... What was Sofia to Nick? Girlfriend? Lover? They'd had two dates. A long, passionate night of sex. Nick straightened, the pain in his side helping him focus. "I'm nowhere near his pocket. In fact, I'd be quite happy if he and Mario had a little talk. One that didn't involve words. What do you know?"

With a grimace, Forlano leaned a hip against his desk. "I own hundreds of people in Boston. Secrets and lies like you wouldn't believe." He chuckled. "Well, perhaps you would. You had plenty of your own secrets, as I recall. I hear things. So do my men. And for the past few months, we've heard rumors of a Russian crew stealing girls off the streets and from clubs and selling them into slavery. They're rounded up over the course of a month or so, then shipped off to somewhere in the motherland where they're sold to private owners or work in brothels.

"The girl—Emily—is Silvio's neighbor. A nice lady, he says.

But she has a wild streak. Drinks and bar hops every weekend. Silvio says he saw some shady characters lurking around the apartment building a few weeks ago. He chased them, but they were too quick for him." With a shake of his head, Damian muttered something about Silvio needing to go on a diet.

"If you know who's taking the girls, why don't you go to the police? I'm sure you have a few in your pocket." Nick's jab landed him against the wall, his left arm bent behind his back. "Fuck! Let me go, you piece of shite."

"Mario." Damian's warning carried a venomous edge, and the enforcer released Nick.

His arm hung half-useless at his side as he rubbed his shoulder to ease the burning pain. Another second or two and the bone would have popped out of the socket.

"I used my contacts on the force. But I'm not the only one with *friends* there. The Human Trafficking Unit is completely under his control. They won't investigate Petrov. They will, however, investigate you."

"Clearly."

"The police consider you a suspect. Victor wants you in his poker game. And you've been seen with one the club's employees." Forlano slid another photo from the file folder. Nick and Sofia outside Artist's Grind.

"Sofia is *not* part of this!" Nick said, his tone bordering on a low growl. "I would bet my life on that fact. Are you having her followed as well? Or just me?"

Damian rolled his eyes. "Just you. For now. Victor's setting you up to take the fall, Nick. I don't know why. Perhaps he's run out of cops he can buy. I haven't figured that out yet. If you want to get out of this situation without going to jail, there's only one way. Work for me."

"When I paid you off, I swore I'd never do business with you again. If you'll excuse me. I'm going to honor that promise." Though he didn't think he'd be successful, Nick turned and tried to slip past Mario. To his shock, the big man moved out of his way, but as Nick reached the door, Mario grabbed the handle and held it shut. "I don't know what you think you're going to get out of me, Damian. Let me go. If Victor's involved with the kidnappings, I have a friend on the force who can find out. But he won't know to look at the guy unless I make it home in one piece."

Nick's steely blue gaze locked on Forlano. Two years ago, the man had scared the piss out of Nick. Now, he wouldn't cower. Eighteen months of twelve-step meetings had taught Nick a lot about who he was, who he wanted to be. Forlano's bitch wasn't high on his list.

"Help us, Nick," the Italian said, his expressionless face seemingly carved out of pure granite. "We want the Russians to leave Boston. *After* they return the girls. Otherwise, we'll go to war. And win. Let Victor pull you into his circle. Then communicate our demands to our mutual...*friend*. Do that, and we'll leave you alone. For now. Cross us, ignore us, and...well...the next bone Mario breaks won't be so small. Or perhaps, it won't belong to you at all."

Mario shoved the phone back into Nick's hands as the town car pulled up to the curb in front of his condo building. "Forlano expects to hear from you by Monday. Don't disappoint him." The big man smiled. "Or do. I'll have fun rearranging your face. I haven't had to hurt anyone lately. Been dying for a good workout."

"Fucker," Nick muttered as the car pulled away. His shoulder throbbed, he still felt the punch to his gut, and now his wrist ached with the memory of the old injury. Once he looked at his phone, he clenched his teeth so hard an instant headache shot up the back of his scalp. Four missed calls. One from Alex and three from Ben.

Nothing from Sofia.

As Nick climbed the stairs, he played Alex's voicemail. "Nicholas, I'm flying back from Seattle with Elizabeth in an hour. I expect you at the house tomorrow at nine. We need to draw up some paperwork protecting Fairhaven Exports and the remainder of your stock in case, as the press seems to believe, the authorities arrest you in the next few days." Alex's voice softened slightly. "I don't believe you had anything to do with that woman's disappearance. Even at your lowest, you still thought of others, and despite some of Candy's poor fashion choices, I know you would never hurt a woman. But you've been reckless and irresponsible, and we need to sever ties for a time. I love you, Nicholas. But I cannot publicly call you family at the moment."

Forgetting all about the calls from Ben, Nick sank into his father's chair, dropped his head into his hands, and wept.

**Sofia**

Tugging at the micro-mini that topped her fishnets, Sofia tried to take a deep breath, but the corset dug into her sides. Gooseflesh rose on her bare shoulders as she stowed her coat and backpack under the bar.

For the moment, she and Leo, the bar manager, were alone in the massive room, the heavy bass of the club's seductive dance mix loud enough to melt her brain. Good. Maybe she'd be able to get through the next few hours without thinking. Much.

Leo sidled over to her. "Last night was dead. I don't know what it is about Thursdays."

"The regulars know I'm off." Sofia scooped up a handful of wood chips and dumped them into one of the bar's garnish bins. Regretting her sharp tongue—even though Leo had always been an ass to her—she sighed. "You've been hounding me for weeks to teach you how to make a smoked cocktail. It's now or never. Pay attention."

Leo watched as she poured a shot of one of her botanical infusions into a cocktail shaker. Next, she dropped a couple of hickory chips into the smoke gun and set them aflame. "Get as much smoke as you can into the snifter," Sofia said. "Then drop a coaster on top while you do the rest."

Once the ghostly vapor started swirling in the snifter, Sofia placed a disposable coaster on top of the glass, aimed the smoke gun into the cocktail shaker for a split second, then simultaneously topped the shaker with a pint glass and extinguished the flame. "Shake well, then pour from a distance. And for fuck's sake, don't try to smoke the hell out of the infusion. You want the drink to have a smoky hint to it, not taste like an ashtray."

Leo took a sip of the concoction. "How'd you learn that?"

"Self-taught. Saw it done at a restaurant once, decided to play around. You've got to have the palate for it. Do *not* deviate from my recipes. Understand?" She gestured to the cheat sheet she'd taped behind the bar.

Though Leo glared at her, he nodded. He might technically be her boss—and a lazy bartender—but he knew what the customers wanted. Her drinks.

As the clock ticked closer and closer to six, Sofia allowed herself the brief hope that Victor wouldn't be in today—or wouldn't come out of his office. But as Wally, one of the bouncers, lumbered towards the front doors, Victor shouted from the hallway.

"Sofia. Get your ass back here."

She flinched, and with a quick glance at Leo, who offered only a smug grin, she headed for the hallway. Trying to force some steel into her spine, she squared her shoulders. *You can do this. Tell Victor Nick's busy and will be in next week. He can't get mad at you for that.*

Victor's close presence behind her—so close she could feel the heat from his body and smell his potent aftershave—was designed to intimidate, but only served to amp her resolve. She'd survived twelve years relying only on her wits and hard work. She'd survive this. Even if Victor made good on this threats.

"Well, *сýка*? Did you do what you were told?" He crossed his arms over his chest as he backed her against his desk and stared down at her, his six-foot-four-inch hulking frame blocking her escape.

"Nick's busy tonight. Prior engagement." Sofia tried to force a harsh edge into her tone, but a hint of a wobble remained. *Shit.* "He'll be in next week."

"That wasn't our agreement."

"What do you want me to do? The man's a billionaire. He's got things to do. Business stuff." She rolled her eyes and rested a hand on her waist, hoping a little attitude would work if confidence didn't. "How the hell did you expect me to get him to cancel all of his plans on one day's notice? Because telling him that you're blackmailing me wouldn't be the smartest way to handle things."

"You little whore." Victor grabbed her by the arms and hauled her up against the wall. Her shoes barely touched the ground, and the shock stole her breath. "If you breathe a word about our discussion to anyone, you will regret ever being born."

"Let me go," she gasped. "I said I'd get him here and I will. Just...not...tonight." Tears gathered at the corners of her eyes. Under his fingers, her arms throbbed, and his hot, sour breath forced her to turn her head or choke.

"Boss?" Leo knocked on the door. As Victor released his grip, Sofia struggled not to let her knees buckle. "Need you to unlock the hard alcohol cabinet for the night. We opened two minutes ago."

With a growl, Victor stalked over to his desk and fished out his keys. Leo caught his toss, then glanced at Sofia. "Got a customer who wants one of your special smoked drinks." Turning to Victor, he arched his brows. "You done with her for now? She's needed behind the bar."

"For now," Victor spat. "But Sofia, I strongly urge you to make a call and have our mutual friend rearrange his schedule. Tonight. Otherwise, I'll have to make a call of my own."

## 16

Sofia

"WHAT THE HELL WAS THAT?" Leo asked as he followed Sofia back to the bar.

She rubbed her arms, thankful for the club's dim lighting and her bronzed skin. If her luck held out, the bruises wouldn't show until the next day. Who was she kidding? Her *luck* had run out hours ago.

"Nothing. He wants me to help him recruit more guys for his poker game. I told him to do his own dirty work." Everyone who had worked at Bound for more than a few months knew about Victor's extracurricular activities, and by unspoken agreement— or because of Victor's threats—they all kept quiet. "He's just angry. He'll get over it. Now, which customer?"

"Huh? I just said that to get you out of there." Leo shook his head. "What?" he asked as Sofia shot him a sideways look. "We might not be friends, but he shouldn't have his hands on you."

Over the music, Sofia caught an odd edge to Leo's voice. Had she misjudged him for the past few years? He'd never been protective before. Though Victor had a couple of inches on the bar manager, Leo's bulk would give him the advantage in a fight.

"Thank you." She tried to hold his gaze, but he shifted his focus to her chest. *Well, there's the asshole I remember.*

"I'm surprised you didn't quit on the spot," he said, then headed for a young woman in a skin-tight latex outfit leaning against the bar. Relieved the awkward moment between them had passed, Sofia grabbed a towel and started scrubbing a water stain on the black marble. She hated that bartending was the best paying job she could get right now. Sexual harassment ran rampant in the restaurant and bar scene, and though she'd love to go to the police and report Victor, her earlier encounter with the cops at Nick's had left a bad taste in her mouth.

The next hour flew by in a flurry of drink orders until Sofia took a quick break, sliding her hip onto a stool behind the bar and sucking down a glass of ice water. Leo kept working, which confused her. Why was the laziest bartender she'd ever met now Mr. Productivity? Once he poured a Sazerac into a rocks glass, he dumped the last sip from the cocktail shaker into a shot glass for himself. Of course. Hard alcohol night. The more drinks he made, the more he could sample.

Someone caught his attention out in the crowd, and Leo jerked his head towards Sofia slightly. But before she could squint into the spotlights, a blond head in her periphery had her shooting to her feet and rounding the bar.

"What the hell are you doing here?" Sofia hissed in Nick's ear. "I told you to stay—"

"Please, love. Get your things and come with me. Right now. I'll explain when we're out of here." Strain pinched his lips and deepened the fine lines around his eyes. He moved gingerly as he wrapped his arm around her waist. "There's a hell of a lot more going on here than merely gambling."

"I can't just leave. I won't get paid—"

"Dammit, Sofia. Trust me," Nick said as he led her towards

the bar. "I'll gladly give you whatever you'll lose by quitting on the spot. Where's your coat? Your bag?"

"No. Stop right now." Sofia wriggled free. "You can't just show up at my job and start ordering me around. We're not in the bedroom." As the words escaped, she realized how ridiculous they sounded given the level of kink surrounding them. Masters led slaves around on leashes. Hard limits night allowed gags, and several subs were blind, mute, and wore large headphones—total sensory deprivation. "Get out of here. If Victor sees you—"

"He's going to wish he never met me," Nick growled. "Or—"

"Sofia, is this guy bothering you?" Wally, one of the bouncers, came up behind her. "I can boot him."

Sofia slapped a hand against Wally's chest. "I'm fine, Wall. Nick's just leaving. He has another event to get to." Trying to smooth things over, she leaned in and brushed her lips to Nick's cheek. "I'll call you when I get off work. I promise. But tonight, you need to trust me."

"At least give me five minutes. Outside," he said as he linked their fingers.

She pressed herself against him. His warmth, his strength, and the desperate edge to his voice softened her resolve.

"Five minutes. Move. Quickly." Sofia glanced back towards the bar and the hallway. No sign of Victor, but the security cameras would have already caught them.

They spilled out onto the sidewalk and Sofia shivered in the cool spring air. Nick wrapped his arm around her, right over the fresh bruises Victor had left. She stifled her wince. Once they'd reached the corner, he met her gaze. "The Forlano crime family believes Victor is running a sex trafficking ring out of the club."

Victor was a dick, but she still couldn't believe he'd be involved with kidnapping and selling young women into slavery. "Poker I get. But...someone else has to be kidnapping those women."

"I'll explain everything when we're not...here. I'm not trying to control you, love. I won't lie. I hate that you had to come back here tonight at all. The man I used to be—before I went into recovery—would have paid your rent for a year without telling you and probably gone directly to Victor and quit for you. Or hell, at least set you up in a better flat where you had your own bedroom." Nick leaned his head against hers. "Of course, he also had rather sizable resources. And a piss-poor track record with relationships. I'm afraid for you, Sofia. If Victor's behind the police sending me up for the kidnapping..."

The police captain. Sofia chewed on her lower lip as she held Nick's gaze for a long moment. "Wait here. I'll get my bag."

Nick hovered by the club door while Sofia wove her way through the crowd, scanning for Victor. As she grabbed her coat and bag from under the bar, Leo grabbed her arm. "What are you doing?"

"Living up to expectations," she said with a wry grin. "I quit." Before she made it more than ten steps, she stopped, turned back to Leo, and rose up on her toes to lean over the bar. "Consider this my thanks for earlier. Get out of here. As soon as you can."

Leaving him with his mouth hanging open, Sofia hurried to the door and into Nick's waiting arms.

**Nick**

Though he had no illusions the police—and Damian Forlano—wouldn't find him if he stayed away from home, some of Nick's tension eased when Sofia asked if they could go to her apartment rather than his condo. She huddled in the passenger seat of his Audi, her backpack clutched tightly in her lap like a shield.

Neither of them spoke until she'd locked her apartment door

behind them. Worry ate away at him. She'd paled, and every few minutes, she'd tug at her corset or rub the back of her neck. Her fingers trembled. "I'm going to change," she whispered once she dumped her backpack on the counter. "I need...a couple of minutes."

Nick paced. Alex was still on a plane, and Ben didn't think they'd find out much more tonight. Not until the lawyer could track down a court clerk willing to reveal the source and timing of the warrant. His phone buzzed, and he cursed as he read Cal's latest text.

*No idea what evidence they have on you. Sitwell shut me out. Put me on desk duty for the next week. Be careful.*

This...going to Bound, being with Sofia...this wasn't careful. But Nick wouldn't leave her tonight if his life depended on it.

*Thanks for trying. Won't lie. Being in Forlano's office, I remember the rush. I'm going to a meeting tomorrow right after I see Alex.*

Sofia emerged, dressed in a black tank, black cardigan, and gray yoga pants. She'd scrubbed off her makeup, and her cheeks held more color. But red rimmed her eyes, and she hugged herself tightly. "I have...um...tea and coffee."

"Let me, love." Nick guided her to the couch with a hand at the small of her back, and when she sank down onto the cushions and grabbed a blanket, pressed a kiss to the top of her head. "Do you take anything in your tea?"

"Honey." She peered up at him, questions in her eyes. "I don't know what to feel. What to do."

"Nor do I." Nick took her hand between both of his, warming her fingers. "Ben and Cal are doing all they can. Tomorrow, I'll enlist Alex's help."

"He's not going to be happy with you," she said with a sad smile.

Reluctantly, Nick let her hand slid from his grip as he backed towards the kitchen. "He's rarely happy with me. Five years apart, remember? We're constantly at odds."

"Not much different from me and Gina." Sofia sniffed, then pulled Nick's handkerchief from the pocket of her cardigan and dabbed at her eyes. "She's seven years younger."

Nick found mugs, the honey, and a tin with Sofia's neat handwriting on the label. "Vanilla chamomile blend? Did you make this yourself?"

At her nod, something inside him broke free. A piece of his heart he'd guarded...possibly forever. They were still new, but Sofia touched him in ways that settled his soul. "You're a treasure," he murmured, too low for her to hear over the whistling kettle.

When he returned to her side with mugs of tea for both of them, she pressed close and rested her head on his shoulder. Sofia jerked when he winced, nearly sloshing tea over the rim of her cup. "Nick? What's wrong? Are you hurt?"

"I spent the afternoon at Damian's Trattoria in the North End. As in Damian Forlano," he said as he rubbed the tender socket. "Head of the Forlano crime family. One of his enforcers didn't much like what I had to say."

"Oh my God." Sofia set down her tea, slid his mug from his hands, and unbuttoned his shirt. Her breath caught in her throat when she pulled the fine cotton open. A reddish lump swelled over his shoulder, and as her hands skimmed down his sides, she caught the edge of the deep purple bruise that darkened above his belt. "Did you call the pol—shit. Never mind. I just realized how ridiculous that sounded. Do you need a doctor?"

He grunted his no as he shifted to pull her into his arms. "I've had worse. Last time I had the good fortune to be his guest for a time, he broke my wrist. I got off easy today."

Sofia trailed her hand down Nick's bare torso. Her touch had the power to heal all of his wounds.

"You said you'd explain. Tell me everything."

## 17

Nick

"You'll need a bit of history, love," he said as he shifted to alleviate some of the pressure on his bruised back. "When the gambling became an addiction rather than a hobby, I ran out of liquid cash."

"Um, aren't you worth billions? Or...weren't you?" Sofia peered up at him, confusion in her warm brown eyes.

"I was. But most of that money was tied up. Stock, investments, retirement funds. My father was careful. Perhaps he knew something about his firstborn's personality." His dry laugh scraped against his raw throat, and he took a long sip of tea. "This is brilliant."

"I like playing with flavors. And...it's cheaper than storebought. You're stalling."

"A little." He met her gaze, terrified she wouldn't accept the truth of his life, of his mistakes. Why should she? She was beautiful, smart, driven. He was a complete fuck-up and had been for quite some time. "I liquidated a significant amount of my holdings. Investment properties around the world, as much of my stock as I could without raising suspicion, several cars..."

"Several? I've never even *owned* a car." Sofia shook her head. "Your life is—was?—so different from mine."

Fuck it if that didn't make him feel worse. Nick tried to shift away, to put some space between him and this woman he feared he loved, but she halted his movement with a hand to his chest. "Stop. If you think I'm going to run or somehow not care about you because you've bought and sold my life's worth a hundred times over"—she shook her head —"okay, a thousand times over, you don't know me very well. If I didn't...care about you, I would have dumped you the second Victor threa—tried to use me to get to you. Keep going."

Nick cupped her cheek. All of his protective, dominant instincts flared, and his voice deepened, strengthened. "When I'm done, you're going to tell me exactly how Victor *threatened* you."

Her lips parted, recognizing a hint of the Master in his tone. "We...both have a lot to explain. Coffee might have been a better choice," she said with a sad smile.

Sofia pulled the blanket up over their legs, and Nick blew out a slow breath. "I ran out of easily accessible cash. I couldn't sell my Fairhaven stock. The board would have gotten wind of it. By this point, I was at the track three times a week and down in Atlantic City every weekend. Derby Weekend was the beginning of the end, I suppose. I'd bet everything I had left on the favorite and the horse broke his leg coming out of the gate. When I settled my account and came up short, a man I'd never seen before stepped up to the window and handed me a stack of cash. 'Yours for a small fee, *signore*.' Twenty-five thousand dollars and all I had to do was pay him back—at a phenomenal interest rate, within two weeks."

Squeezing the back of his neck to try to release some of the tension, Nick continued. "Within six months, I'd amassed a debt of almost a million."

"Oh my God."

"I kept losing." Nick offered her a rueful smile. "That's the addiction. It lies to you: 'Just one more bet. You'll win this one. It's a sure thing.'" Another sip of tea provided him the courage to admit the worst of it. "You know about the trouble Alex and Elizabeth had when they started dating? The men who were after her?"

"Yes. Even with my head buried in a text book and just starting at Bound, I read about *that*. Everyone did. Hell, I think that was the American equivalent of the Royal Baby watch."

His laugh shattered some of the stress clamped around his chest. "Something like that, yeah. That cock-up put Fairhaven Exports' financials all over the news the week before Christmas. And Forlano ran out of patience. He threatened me several times, and I cobbled together fifty thousand dollars as a down payment with a promise that he'd get the rest of his money by the first of the year. That's when he had one of his goons break my wrist. Then they came to see me at my office—and manhandled Elizabeth. Alex was furious. Rightfully so. Hell, she'd just escaped a hitman. Alex almost died. And she was hurt—again—because of me. I confessed everything to him that night, agreed to enter a twelve-step program, and he paid my entire debt the next day."

Sofia blew out a breath. "A million dollars in a single day?"

Shame crashed over Nick like a tidal wave. He stared down at Sofia's hand on his. "Damian Forlano owned me for six months. I would have done anything he asked—and he knew it. As did Alex."

"How does this all relate to what's going on at Bound, though?" Sofia's brows drew together, and Nick pressed a kiss to the little furrow.

"The Forlano family owns this city. They have for generations. I don't know all the details, but a little less than a year ago, they heard rumblings about the Russians moving in. Pushing drugs, getting young, pretty women hooked on heroin, then selling them and shipping them off to other countries to work the sex trade. Forlano's an ass. He'll prey on your biggest weakness to get what he wants, and if you don't give in, he'll break bones until you do. But the man respects women." Nick snorted. "You should have seen his face when he told me what was going on. The disgust. The rage. He saw the police reports naming me a suspect. I'm surprised he didn't have me drowned in the Harbor on sight.

"I don't know why he believed me." Nick ran a hand through his hair, Forlano's threats echoing in his ears. "Or maybe he's just that desperate. Emily—the girl I tried to save—she's one of his enforcer's neighbors. He wants her back and—" he laughed. "The man actually asked for my help. Told me to get involved with Victor and see what I could find out about the girls. Either that, or he's going to start a war."

"You're not...?"

"No." Nick twined their fingers again. "I won't gamble again. I can't. But I do have to see what I can find out about Victor. Perhaps see if I can get close to him."

"How many other girls?" Worry painted Sofia's lovely features, and Nick's heart felt two sizes too big for his chest.

"At least four that Damian knows about. Cal—my sponsor— he was investigating the disappearances until someone convinced the police they should focus their investigation on me. But his captain knows we're friends, and he's put Cal on desk duty."

Sofia drew back, her lips pressed into a thin line, shoulders hunched. "What does Cal look like?"

"Why?"

An invisible weight pressed down on her, stealing the vibrant passion in her eyes. She sighed, wrapped her arms around herself, and pulled her legs up under the blanket. "Because Victor has at least two city officials *and* a police captain in his back pocket. That's what he tried to use to get me to bring you into the poker game. He said if I didn't succeed, the cop would fabricate a police record for me—a felony—and I'd never work again."

**Sofia**

As Sofia recounted her conversations with Victor, she tried to keep a handle on her emotions, but by the time she'd finished, her eyes burned with unshed tears. At least Nick had confirmed that the police officer she'd seen wasn't his sponsor. Cal was older, had more of a gut, and apparently always smelled like onions, stale coffee, and Christmas trees. He'd also burned one of his hands in the line of duty, and the scars were obvious.

"Why is this happening?" She dabbed at her eyes with Nick's handkerchief, which by now was half-soaked. "I just wanted a good job. One where I didn't get groped every night. One that would let me save up enough to pay for school. How did I end up working for someone who could *sell* women?"

Nick rose and started to pace her small living room. "I want to know why he was so keen on getting me into the poker game. What the fuck does that have to do with the missing women?"

Her tea long cold, Sofia slumped against the cushions. "Maybe he wanted to make sure you were at the club every night. You wouldn't have an alibi."

"True." Leaning against her kitchen counter, Nick called Cal. "I'm sorry for ringing so late. But I'm here with Sofia. Victor has a police captain in his pocket. She didn't get his name. What does Sitwell look like?"

Nick relayed Cal's description, and Sofia breathed a small sigh of relief. "No. This guy was bigger. Maybe fifty-five, balding. Had a thick Boston accent and very trim," she said.

Putting the phone on speaker, Nick returned to her side as the sound of computer keys came over the line. "It could be the captain of District A-7. But not everyone has their bio online. I'll send you a link to Captain Usher's page. Though even if we find out who it is...I don't know what we'd do about it. Without hard evidence, something more concrete than Sofia's testimony, there's no way Sitwell would believe me."

"So what should I—we—do?" Nick asked as he wrapped his arm around Sofia's shoulders. Even knowing how much trouble they might be in, she took comfort from his strong embrace. Being cared for felt foreign. Her entire adult life, she'd been the one doing the caring. Even her previous Master hadn't made her feel as safe and protected as Nick did. Norm had been new to BDSM at the time, and though they enjoyed several months together, she'd never once thought about a real future with him.

"I don't know, Nick. Lay low for tonight. I'll call one of my sketch artist buddies in the morning. If Sofia can describe the guy she met, maybe we'll have something. Until then, be careful."

Once Nick ended the call, he sighed and glanced around her tidy space. "This couch pulls out?"

"Yes. You're willing...to stay here?" Shock lent a breathiness to her tone, and she fiddled with the hem of her sweater. "It's...not the most comfortable mattress. I thought...you'd want to go home."

Nick nudged her chin up so she met his gaze. "I want to be wherever you are tonight. And you're here. I'm knackered, love. I can sleep anywhere as long as I know you're with me—and safe. Or, at least as safe as I can make you." Gesturing to the curtain tied back against the wall, he raised a brow. "Privacy screen?"

With a nod, Sofia rose and drew the curtain across the room. "Not that we'll need it. Gina's down in Atlantic City somewhere with a guy she just met three days ago. She's getting all of her rebelling done in the space of a week. By the time she gets on the plane, I might not even recognize her anymore."

"I hope you'll introduce me before she leaves." Nick moved to her side and sunk his fingers into her hair. "If this whole bloody mess has shown me anything, love, it's that I want you in my life. This isn't a fling for me. I don't think it ever was."

Sofia held her breath as he leaned in to brush his lips to hers. She couldn't get enough of the taste of him, the way he held her, the way she felt whenever they touched. His tongue teased the seam of her lips, and she slid her arms up to wrap them around his neck. Nick tugged at her hair, the pinpricks of pain along her scalp flooding her with arousal. Moaning, she ground her hips against him, and he cupped her ass, lifting her so she could wrap her legs around his waist.

"I don't have any of my usual toys here," he said as he nuzzled her neck. "I don't suppose you have anything we could use?"

"I...uh...have a box under the couch." Sofia squirmed as he carried her back to the couch, and once he'd set her down, she retrieved the blue box of toys.

Nick lifted the lid and grinned. "Well, this is quite the collection."

As he withdrew the silk and hemp rope, the new vibrating butt plug, and the leather flogger, Sofia tried not to blush. "I might have picked up a few things between interviews," she admitted.

"A few things." He blew out a breath. "These are very nice indeed." Brushing the rope against her cheek, he asked, "What do you want, kitten?"

"Tie me up, Sir."

His lips curved into a predatory grin. "I have to undress you first." Nick's fingers blazed a path along the collar of her tank to her shoulders. The cardigan slipped down her arms, trapping them at her sides, and he chuckled. "This...might do for a few minutes." Snatching the bottom of the long sweater, he tied a loose knot at her waist. "I won't stretch this too much, will I?"

"N-no. It's ancient." With her arms immobile, she couldn't

touch him. She tried to sit up, but he gently pressed her against the cushions.

"No moving, kitten. I'm in control now. What's your safe word?"

Nick held her gaze until she said, "Red," then cupped the back of her neck and claimed her mouth. His kiss stole all rational thought. When he pinched her nipple, hard, she whimpered and arched her back, trying to find some friction against her sensitive nub. That earned her another pinch to the other breast and a warning growl as he broke the kiss.

"You're dancing close to a punishment, Sofia." Nick's stormy blue eyes churned, the whiskey-colored flecks dancing with excitement and desire. "I can't say that would upset me."

"What...would I have to do to cross that line, Sir?" Trying to scoot closer, she played coy as long as she could, but from the look on his face, he saw right through her. "I...I want you to hurt me, Sir. I need you to punish me. Take me. Please. You are my Master, and I trust you. No one has ever made me feel like you do..."

For a long moment, neither of them moved. Something more swirled in his eyes now, something she thought just might be love. Nick sucked in a breath, swallowed hard, and trailed the backs of his fingers along her cheek. "You will feel everything tonight, Sofia. Pleasure and pain. You undo me. Are you ready to begin?"

"Yes, Sir. I'm ready."

# 18

**Nick**

NICK RAN his hands down Sophia's body. His sweet sub surprised him every day. He wondered if she knew how much she affected him.

She wriggled as his fingers danced closer to her mound. He would have to bind her soon. But first, he would torture her a little. Make her beg. And only then, would he grant her release. Little mewls and moans escaped her lips as he teased her breasts and feathered kisses along her collarbone. "I'm just getting started, love. And I can tell you're already soaked for me."

Inhaling deeply, the scent of her arousal driving him half mad, he skimmed his teeth along the shell of her ear. With a whimper, she bucked her hips. "Please, Sir. I need..."

"What do you need?" Pressing closer to her, he tugged the low-cut tank down with one hand and cupped a breast with the other. Shite. She wasn't wearing a bra. "Good girl," he said as he skated his thumb over her nipple and she struggled against the sweater wrapped around her arms. "But you're still wearing too many clothes."

"So...take them...off me..." A little smile teased him until she sucked her lower lip between her teeth and fought not to cry out. "These walls...are thin..." Each word escaped on a gasp, and she locked her gaze on his, pleading.

"I don't have my gag, love."

"Scarf. Coat rack."

Nick sprinted for the door, found the scarf and the belt from her coat, and returned to his sub. Nick covered her lips with his as he rolled the nipple between his fingers, and when she cried out again, his kiss absorbed much of the sound. "We'll save the gag for a bit. At least until my tongue is busy elsewhere."

He gave equal attention to the other breast and desperation infused Sofia's movements. So expressive, so very responsive, and he'd not even removed her pants yet. The loose knot in her sweater unraveled when he pressed a kiss to her mound, and she fought her way out of the sleeves. He let her have her little rebellion. He'd punish her soon enough.

And now, he had easy access to remove her tank. How convenient. Her breasts bared to him, Nick laved his tongue over first one nipple, then the other, freeing his hands to cup her hips and drag her lower on the couch. Fuck, she was perfect in every way. He kissed a trail down her stomach, and, tugging at her waistband, had the pants off her in a single tug.

A black lace thong did nothing to contain her arousal. The apex of her thighs glistened with need. His first taste sent his own desires soaring, and if he wasn't careful, he'd tear the lace from her body without a second thought.

Writhing almost off the couch, Sofia grabbed fistfuls of his hair. "Please, Sir. I need your mouth on me."

"Who gives the orders in the bedroom, kitten?" Nick said and then bit down over her lace-covered clit.

With a yelp, she squeaked, "You do, Sir. But..."

"I'm afraid you've earned a punishment. But...as you're

currently so wanton I don't think you can stand...give me your hands."

He tried to hide his smile as she obeyed. Nick folded the rope in half, grabbed the center, and wound the silky braid around first one wrist, then the other.

"Sir?" she said as she focused on the half-foot of space between her wrists. "How is this...?"

"Shh, kitten." Nick worked quickly, his cock throbbing with need for his sub. When he finished, he'd approximated a short wrist spreader by coiling the rope around and around the length between her two hands. Sofia couldn't bring her hands together or separate them, and she ground her hips against the couch as he lifted her bound wrists over her head.

Tying a knot around the thick coils of rope, he let the belt fall behind the couch. "Don't move, kitten."

She obeyed as he sank to the floor on his knees, retrieved the end of the belt, and tied it to her left ankle. Stepping back, he admired how lovely she looked tied to her couch. The position put an arch in her back, and her breasts thrust forward.

"Sir...gag me..."

The last word died in her throat as Nick pulled the lace thong down her legs and ran his tongue through her slick folds. Her essence, the very taste of Sofia flooded him. He held her thighs wide, parting her lower lips so he could trace patterns on the bundle of nerves that would send her over the edge into ecstasy.

"Are you sure?" Nick sat next to her, the scarf in his hands. "Wool isn't the most comfortable gag."

"I'll...scream."

Tying the thin, green scarf around her head, he brushed a gentle kiss to her parted lips. He snagged his keys from the coffee table and pressed them into her hands. "If you need to safeword, kitten, drop the keys. I'll hear them fall. Do you understand?"

She nodded, and the need in her eyes drove him towards the

edge of his own control. Returning his focus to her mound, he drank in her essence.

With every movement, she flew higher. Her legs trembled with the effort of holding back her release. Emotion swelled in his chest. He hadn't told her not to come, but she knew his desires now, his rhythm. His heart. A tremor along her sides told him she wouldn't be able to hold on much longer. He paused long enough to give her permission. "Come for me, Sofia."

Nick thrust his tongue against her clit and Sofia flew apart. The scream that escaped her lips—even muffled by the gag— would certainly reach the neighbors, but let them come knocking. He didn't care. Her release coated his lips, his tongue, even his chin, and he lapped up every bit he could until, over-sensitized, she started to whimper.

"Shhh, love." Nick freed the belt that tied her to the couch and gathered her against him, her naked body still trembling. "I've got you. Arms over my head now." He loosed the gag, pulling the damp scarf from between her teeth.

"Uh-huh," she murmured as she tucked her head against his neck. "Don't...let go."

Pressing a kiss to the top of her head, he whispered, "Never."

**Sofia**

"Shall we try out some of these other...toys?"

Nick's deep voice in her ear brought her back from wherever she'd gone after her release. Somewhere warm and secure that smelled like him. Sofia blinked hard to focus, and his smug smile coalesced in front of her. "I'd like that, Sir."

"Brilliant. Do you think you can stand?" Nick brushed a curl away from her face. She stretched her legs, the delicious ache in her pussy leaving her feeling languid, yet a part of her was still pulled taut. She felt as if she would snap at any moment.

Sofia nodded. "I think so, Sir."

"Bend over the couch."

He helped her, massaging her arms and back as he slid his hands up and down her body. When she had her knees on the cushions and her breasts pressed to the back of the couch, Nick coated the new butt plug with lube and gently pressed the silicone against the rosebud of her ass.

"I've never..." she whispered, and he paused. "But with you...I want this, Sir."

His lips brushed her ear. "Are you sure? Ass play can be intense, love."

"Please." She tugged at the wrist restraints, the firm bindings slipping gently over her skin, but not giving enough for her to do more than move her fingers or bend her elbows. "I want you to own me completely, Sir. Tonight, more than ever. I need this."

He rested his cheek against her bare shoulder. "You are perfect, kitten. I'm—" With a sigh, he kissed the back of her neck before the firm pressure against her ass quickened her breath and made her squirm. "Bear down, but relax as much as possible."

She did, and the pop as the toy breached her brought pain, but also a delicious fullness she'd never experienced before. "Oh God. Yes."

With the remote in his hand, Nick guided her back to her feet. "Feel all right?" Concern darkened his stormy gaze.

Sofia nodded. "Green, Sir. Very green."

Leading her over to the far wall, he gestured to a hook mounted close to the ceiling. "For a bike?"

"It's rated for a hundred pounds." Sofia shivered, gooseflesh rising along her arms, her back, and her ass. Nick looped the belt over the hook and tied it to the column of rope between her wrists so her arms were taut above her head.

"I still owe you a punishment, kitten." Nick rummaged around the box until he found her vibrator. "Oh, very nice." He held up the u-shaped piece of silicone. "Charged, I assume?"

"As of two weeks ago..."

Nick snagged her thong from the floor. Striding over to her, he kissed her until she couldn't breathe. "Please, Sir," she whispered. Her lips tingled. He stooped and lifted first one of her feet, then the other to help her back into her thong. "What are you—?"

"Remember, love. I'm in control here. Are you still at green?" His lips and tongue blazed a lazy path up her thigh, to her stomach, each breast, and behind her left ear.

"Green," she confirmed, though she ached for him. For his cock to fill her. For him to cover her body with his. "Oh!" she cried as he tucked the vibrator inside her channel. Her thong held the silicone in place, one nub deep inside her pressing against her g-spot and the other half resting on her clit.

Nick stepped back, his gaze roving up and down her body. "You are stunning, Sofia. So beautiful. Strong." He held up the vibrator's remote and, with a wicked smile, pressed the button.

Her body came alive, the twin vibrations propelling her to the edge of another release before Nick even dropped his hand. "You will *not* come, kitten. Not if you want me to redden that ass of yours before I take you."

*Oh God.*

Sofia squirmed, but the belt held her in place. If she could just get a little more friction between her legs...but she *needed* the pain. Needed Nick to be the one to give her the exquisite agony that marked her as his. As cared for. As...loved.

The couch folded out with a groan, and the vibrator fell

silent. So close she could taste her release, Sofia tried to force a slow, deep breath from her lungs. "Please...Sir. I can't hold on."

Nick took his time making the bed. The vibrator kept her squirming. On just long enough to send her racing towards the edge of oblivion, then off until she begged him to let her come.

"Soon, love. I promise." Nick stripped off his shirt, and as he approached, he activated the vibrator in her ass.

Sofia screamed, then bit down her lip to stifle the sound. He set a random pattern; she didn't know if she would fly apart or implode. "Are you ready for me to punish you?"

"God, yes. Please," she begged, tugging harder at the ropes around her wrists. The smooth rope slid over her skin, and the delicious sensations drove her higher. "Sir..."

Nick spun her around. His hands on her ass, along with the random on-again-off-again pattern of the butt plug and the slow burn of the vibrator in her pussy kept her teetering on the edge of control. The scarf once more slipped between her teeth, and he pressed his keys into her palm.

"You will *not* come," he practically growled in her ear, and then the heat of his body vanished, and the flogger snapped against his palm.

The first strike landed across her ass and Sofia screamed. The second hit the backs of her thighs. He alternated strikes, the intensity, the pattern—all while playing with the vibrators and telling her how beautiful she was, how perfect, how he loved watching her wriggle and squirm.

Flames consumed her ass. Her core was so tight she feared she'd snap in two at any moment. And then...he stopped.

"The next time you're in my bed, kitten, you'll know what total and complete restraint is." With a tug, he released the gag, then the belt, and caught her in his arms.

Carrying her over to the bed, he smiled down at her, his own need etched on his face. She tried to reach down and adjust the vibrator, knowing he'd stop her. When he dipped his head and sucked one pert nipple into his mouth, she arched her back, desperate.

Her release barreled closer, but too soon, cold air hit her breast. "On your knees."

Despite his command, he helped her kneel on a cushion, though when her ass hit her heels, she hissed. "I need...to come... Sir," she begged.

"So do I."

Sofia licked her lips as Nick shed his pants and briefs. His cock jutted proudly amid trim blond curls, and he tangled his fingers in her hair. "You're a treasure, kitten. Shite," he groaned as she took him deep, her bound hands resting on her thighs.

Sofia licked, sucked, and hummed as he thrust his hips. She loved the taste of him, the feel of his silky, smooth skin, the way his balls slapped against her chin as she brought him closer to his climax.

"Fuck," he managed as he pulled away. "You could do that all night long, and I'd die a happy man. But I want to come inside you. Lie down."

Once he'd yanked off her thong and removed the vibrator in her pussy, he sheathed himself. Sofia parted her legs, and with one thrust, he filled her so completely, she couldn't tell where she ended and he began. "You're mine, love. My heart," he whispered as he touched his forehead to hers. "I may never let you go."

"Don't, Sir. I'm yours."

He took up a punishing rhythm. Her bruised, reddened, and plugged ass sliding against the rough sheets, the scent of them, together, all around her, and the way his cock rasped against her sensitive nub brought her once more to a place where nothing existed but bursts of light and color behind her eyes, the roar of her own heartbeat in her ears, and Nick.

With a click, the butt plug turned on again, and the two of them cried out together as the sensation consumed her.

"Sofia!" He shuddered and tweaked her clit as his release overtook him, his cock swelling, and the spasms sending her over the edge until nothing existed but pleasure and pain and oblivion.

## 19

Nick

THE ROUGH, unfamiliar sheets scraped over his naked body, but the scent of Sofia and the hours they'd shared before collapsing into a dreamless sleep centered him. He forced his eyes open to find his raven-haired beauty sprawled next to him, one arm curled around his waist, the other flung across the bed. She lay on her stomach, her lovely, reddened ass curving gracefully with the sheets pooled around her thighs.

The first light of dawn sliced through the drapes, casting the sparse room in a golden glow. Nick eased out from under her arm, relieved when she didn't stir. Four fingertip bruises marred her delicate skin and anger burned deep inside him. In a previous life—one in which he wasn't publicly disgraced—he'd find Victor Petrov and give the man a few bruises of his own. Instead, he'd do the next best thing. Phone in hand, he headed for Sofia's kitchen and, as quietly as he could, prepared her coffee maker as he scanned his messages. Alex had apparently been up for an hour already and expected him in two hours. He bristled at being *summoned* by his younger brother, but he needed Alex's help.

Damian Forlano's as well. He texted the number he'd used so many times when he'd been gambling and the itch to place a bet crawled up his spine. He needed a meeting. Unfortunately, his psychological needs came far behind his need to protect Sofia and clear his name.

*Forlano, Victor has a cop working for him. Don't know who.*

Coffee started to drip into the pot, and across the room, Sofia murmured something unintelligible and rolled over as Damian replied.

*If that stronzo thinks the police are his, he's going to find out he's sorely mistaken. Have you delivered my message yet?*

Nick ran a hand through his hair. He had five texts from Ben warning him that any contact with Forlano wouldn't look good if the police decided to aggressively pursue the kidnapping charges against him, but Nick didn't know where else to turn. After learning about the police captain, he'd tried to hide his dismay from Sofia. With Cal relegated to the sidelines, and most of Boston convinced Nick was a proper fuck-up, he didn't have much of a choice. The only way to protect the sleeping woman across the room was to make sure Victor went to jail for his crimes.

He was either making the biggest mistake of his life or he was bloody brilliant. Given his track record—he grimaced at the poor choice of words—this wouldn't end well. But what else could he do? With a sigh, he replied to Damian.

*No. Victor threatened my girlfriend. I had to make sure she was safe before I went to see him. I'm headed there this afternoon. But I need you to ask around and get me the name of the police captain who frequents Victor's poker games.*

As Nick poured a mug of coffee, the mobster replied.

*Watch your tone. I don't work for you. But I will see what I can dig up.*

As the caffeine kicked in, Nick sat next to Sofia. Sunlight illuminated streaks of auburn in her black hair, and he gently traced the edges of a curl. "I think I love you, Sofia," he whispered. "Which is why I have to go."

Minutes later, he set a note on the pillow next to her, pressed a gentle kiss to her cheek, and then slipped out the door.

Alex's home always reminded him of what he'd lost. The two-story, mid-century-modern architecture was common in the wealthier neighborhoods of Boston. This time of year, flowers bloomed around the twin columns on either side of the porch and the season's first roses graced the yard. Samuel, Alex's household manager and longest-serving employee, answered the bell.

"Welcome, sir. Mr. Fairhaven is expecting you." The terse edge to Samuel's voice worried Nick. Despite the man's complete loyalty to Alex, he was a consummate professional at all times. Nick had seen him be pleasant to the worst of the local reporters.

"Is everything all right, Samuel?" Nick asked as he handed over his coat.

"Fine, sir. Mr. Fairhaven is in his office. I trust you know the way." Samuel hung Nick's coat, then immediately turned and headed for the stairs.

Worry tightened a band across Nick's chest. Elizabeth. Something had to be wrong with Elizabeth for Samuel to rush off like that.

Nick didn't bother knocking on Alex's office door before he burst in. "What's wrong?"

Dark circles bruised Alex's eyes. More worrisome, creases and wrinkles marred his shirt, and he hadn't shaved.

"No hello?" Alex rubbed his eyes. "The trip was dreadful in

every way. Elizabeth's father passed away several days ago, and her mother made a horrible scene at the funeral."

"Bloody hell. That's not all, though. I know you, brother. And how you feel about Elizabeth's mother. You probably bought her company out from under her no more than five minutes after whatever scene she made. What else is wrong?" Nick sank into a chair across from Alex and leaned forward, his arms braced against the desk. "Is Elizabeth all right?"

For a moment, the strife and tension between the two of them fell away. Alex's hands balled into fists on his desk, and he squeezed his eyes shut. "Elizabeth was pregnant."

*Was.*

"Fuck. Alex, I'm sorry."

His brother opened his eyes, his gaze so like the young boy he'd been so many years ago, pleading for his older brother to fix some problem, hide the candy their father slipped them on weekends, or save him from a bully. Gone was the CEO, the feared negotiator, the cocky billionaire. In his place, worry and grief combined to leave Alex a shell of his usual self.

"The stress of the trip...of losing her father...they contributed, of course. But she passed out a few minutes after her mother slapped her and told her she never wanted to see Elizabeth again." Alex's voice cracked, and he slammed his fist down on his desk. "Her doctor says she'll be fine, that there's no lasting damage, that we can try again in a few months. But she's barely spoken to me since we left Seattle."

Nick dropped his head into his hands. A baby. No wonder Alex looked so shattered. He thought back to Lia's death and their father's passing. Grief threatened to choke him, but he swallowed hard and forced himself to meet Alex's gaze. "Elizabeth's grieving. So are you. Remember how Mum was after Father died? They'd divorced more than ten years prior, but still...she refused to speak to anyone for two weeks."

Nick reached across the desk and grasped his brother's arm.

"Elizabeth needs time. But...she needs you as well." An uneasy feeling churned in his gut. "You look like you slept in your clothes."

Guilt pinched Alex's features. "She asked to be alone. She won't even let me hold her at the moment. I slept in a chair. Space I'll give her. But she knew expecting me to sleep in the guest room was folly. Though listening to her cry half the night when I could do nothing but hide my own tears—" Alex clenched his fists, the battle for control of his emotions playing over his haggard face. "I don't know what to do for her."

Alex pulled away and scrubbed his hands over his face, but not before Nick caught the glisten of moisture in his brother's eyes.

"You talk to her." A narrowed gaze pinned Nick, but this...he knew something about grief that Alex hadn't yet learned. "She's in pain. As are you. No one in the world is going to be able to understand what Elizabeth is going through better than you. Grieve *with* her. Not down here alone. And for fuck's sake, don't hide your feelings from her." Nick offered a dry laugh. "You hate giving up control. But grief is a much stronger Master than you'll ever be. Don't try to rein it in. You'll just end up like me."

His brother's emerald green eyes flickered with a hint of understanding. Perhaps for the first time, he had an idea how grief led Nick astray.

After a long minute of silence, Alex sighed. "Ben kept me informed while we were gone." When he met Nick's gaze again, the need for reassurance was gone. Now, the head of the Fairhaven family stared back at him. "Explain to me why you didn't leave Damian Forlano's restaurant and go directly to the police."

"Sofia."

One of Alex's trim brows arched. "Sofia? The woman you're dating. What does she have to do with this?"

Half an hour later, Nick blew out a breath as he flopped
against the back of the chair. "I'm fucked, Alex. As is Sofia. She
did nothing wrong. Other than accepting a ride home from me
after a long night. What am I supposed to do? Just leave her to the
wolves? I..." Nick's voice cracked. "I think I love her."

"Are you sure she's not involved with this whole mess?"

Jumping to his feet, Nick slammed his palms on the desk.
"You're walking a very narrow line right now, brother. I'll forget
you said that because I know you're grieving and worried about
Elizabeth, but I'll also remind you that not too long ago, you
asked *me* to trust you when the woman *you* were dating turned
out to be involved in an embezzlement scheme that could have
cost our company billions."

"And I believe you asked me the same question back then."
Alex's cool, calm demeanor unnerved Nick, so he turned and
started to pace.

"Forlano's supposed to be looking into the cop Victor has on
the take. Once I get a name, maybe Cal...?"

"I know someone in the FBI." Alex pinched the bridge of his
nose. "He's an arse. But he's based out of the New York office, so
he wouldn't have any connections to the Boston Police Department. I'll call him and see if he can offer any advice. But in order
to keep the board happy, Nicholas, I need to ask for your permanent resignation. No more leave of absence."

Nick's mouth went dry, and he stared at Alex like his brother
had grown another head. "I've turned my life around in the past
eighteen months." Dipping his hand into his pocket, Nick
fumbled for his chip. Finding only a couple of quarters, he
frowned, trying to remember the last time he'd had the damn
thing. "In case you haven't noticed, I'm active with several chari-

ties. Before this fucking mess, I'd stayed out of the papers for more than a year. I've met every single one of the board's demands, as ridiculous as some of them were."

"Nicholas." Alex slid a sealed envelope across his desk. "The board's next meeting is in ten days. By then, this situation has to be resolved. Or you'll sign these papers."

Betrayal sliced through Nick's heart and the envelope crumpled in his grip. "I know we haven't been close in quite some time, but we're family, and family is supposed to stick together."

"What do you think I'm doing?" Standing, Alex shoved his hands into his pockets and wandered over to the window. Staring at the street outside, his voice took on a weary tone. "I bought you ten days. And persuaded the more vocal members of the board to make the ultimate choice yours. Not theirs. They were ready to vote you out yesterday with no recourse. Not even a phone call informing you of the vote."

*Oh.*

"Thank you." Nick's quiet apology caught in his throat and he smoothed the wrinkles in the envelope. "I need a meeting. Right after my appointment with Ben. But...is there anything I can do for you? Or Elizabeth?"

"Give us time."

Despite the obvious dismissal, Nick clapped a hand on his brother's shoulder. Alex turned, tears lining his eyes. Nick didn't speak, just wrapped his arms around his brother and let the man cry.

## 20

**Sofia**

PAPER CRINKLED as she rolled over. Nick's scent lingered in the room, but when she opened her eyes, she found the bed empty. What time was it?

Her eyes bleary, she snagged her phone from the side table. "Oh my God." How could she have slept past ten in the morning? Her sister's absence, the stress from the previous night, and the hours of intense sex had sent her into a dreamless, deep sleep.

*Sofia,*
*I'm sorry I couldn't make you breakfast this morning. Particularly since my last attempt failed so miserably. I found a travel mug in the cabinet and left you coffee. I hope it's still hot when you wake. I have to see Alex this morning and I have an idea that might give us some peace of mind. Please stay home today. Don't go back to Bound. I'll be in touch by early afternoon, and we'll figure out what to do next.*
*Love,*
*Nick*

Love. That word warmed her down to her toes, even as a part of her bristled at being told to stay home. Still, he hadn't said "I love you." Was his "Love, Nick" simply a formality? A tender way to sign off, scribbled without a thought? And if not...did she love him back?

She grabbed her phone and sent him a text.

*Going to study all day. In case Victor hasn't totally fucked up my life. I won't leave. Text me when you can. <3*

The little emoji was a cop-out, but she couldn't bring herself to type out the words. A few minutes later, as she sipped the coffee he'd left her, the phone buzzed.

*I won't let him, love. I promise.*

No amount of reassurance could convince her they'd escape this situation unscathed, but as long as she could work...somewhere...and Nick didn't end up in jail, maybe they'd be okay. Maybe they'd have a future and be able to say those three little words to one another.

Sometime during their play the previous night, Sofia's emotions had tipped over the edge from care and affection to love. So why hadn't she told him? Hell, she'd never said those words to anyone—not in that way. But when she thought of Nick, her heart filled to bursting. Every time.

Scrolling through her messages, she frowned. Gina hadn't texted her since yesterday morning. Gina always checked in. Until she'd met Rick. Shit. Sofia hoped Rick wasn't getting her baby sister hooked on whatever had been in that little baggie.

*Gina, please let me know you're alive. I quit my job, and I'll be home all day.*

She couldn't blame Gina for having some fun. After all, that's what she'd been doing. Her ass and thighs still burned and she rubbed the tender flesh. Wandering into the bathroom, Sofia turned on the shower. Naked, she twisted to examine her backside. She couldn't wait until they could go back to his place. She

ached to feel his flogger on her bare skin again and maybe...
more. Her prior BDSM experiences had been limited to a single
Master learning his own ropes, and though she'd not encoun-
tered any hard limits—other than darkness—she'd seen enough
at Bound she wanted to try but had never found anyone she
trusted with her pleasure.

As Sofia stepped under the hot water, she wondered how far
this smart, sexy, and oh-so-dominant man had fallen for her.

**Nick**

As he locked his car, he rang Cal. "Where are you, mate? I'm a
couple of blocks from St. Augustine's." The standing 2:00 p.m.
Saturday GA meeting had been one of Nick's mainstays at the
start of his recovery, and he didn't think he could get through the
day without some grounding. He'd learned little in the hours
he'd been away from Sofia and after the tirade Ben loosed on him
for going to Bound the previous night—he'd been photographed,
again—Nick's nerves were raw.

"I can't make it." Cal huffed out a breath. "Sitwell's riding my
ass on some paperwork and then I've got to take Hannah up to
New York City to see her family. You have no idea how much I
need to get out of here, but if I leave early, he'll probably suspend
me. I have a call out to the sketch artist I told you about, but he
hasn't gotten back to me."

"You need a new job." Nick jabbed the crossing light, then like
any self-respecting Bostonian, gave it a two-count and jogged
across the street anyway. "I'm headed back to Sofia's after the
meeting, though we might go to a hotel for the night. I don't like

the idea of anyone knowing where to find us. Not until Forlano gets back to me."

"Did your brother offer any assistance?" The strain in Cal's voice lent a raspy tone to the question. "He's pretty influential in this town. Doesn't he have a few friends in the department?"

Nick sighed. "Alex has his own problems to deal with at the moment. And as he and the board are lobbying to have me permanently removed... I'm lucky he didn't kick me out of his house this morning." In truth, Alex had been more than fair in light of the loss he'd suffered. Though Nick had shared the very worst of himself with Cal, he wouldn't divulge Alex's secrets to anyone.

Cal whistled. "Wow. That's..."

"Alex has his reasons," Nick said quietly. "But that's why I need a meeting. I'm turning off my phone and heading inside. This group tends to run long, so I'll be off the grid for ninety minutes or so. Let me know if you hear anything about the sketch artist."

"Will do. Call me when you're done."

Nick ended the call. He ached to hear Sofia's voice, but if he rang her now, he wouldn't go inside. He'd probably end up back at her apartment, scratching the itch to gamble by losing himself pleasuring her lovely body. And while that would certainly be enjoyable, the craving currently burning inside him would only grow until he couldn't fight anymore.

Turning off his phone, he hoped her day had been better than his. The church rec room smelled of coffee and doughnuts, and as Nick shoved his hands into his pockets, missing the feel of the chip between his fingers, a woman with an eager smile and bright red hair welcomed him. "Hi. I'm Alice."

## Sofia

A knock on her door roused her, and Sofia jerked, the psychology textbook tumbling to the floor. Despite how late she'd slept, spending hours going over the dry, technical material had left her sorely in need of caffeine. Or perhaps, Nick. As she staggered towards the door, nerves churned in her belly. She wasn't expecting anyone.

"Yes?" she called as she peered through the peephole.

"Miss Oliviera? I have a delivery from a Mr. Fairhaven? Takeout from Señor Cho's," the smiling older man said as he hefted a brown paper bag.

"Oh!" Sofia threw open the door. The scents of chow mein and enchiladas wafted over her. The little restaurant a few blocks away had changed hands half a dozen times over the years, and the latest owner had opted for a Chinese and Mexican fusion menu that could cure almost anything. "Thank you," she said as she accepted the bag. "Let me get you a tip."

"Thank you, miss."

Two steps towards her kitchen counter, a stinging pain in her neck knocked the bag from her fingers, and as the world slowed, the ground rushed up to meet her.

"I'm sorry, kid," the man said as he knelt next to her and smoothed a hand over her hair. His breath stank of onions and his cologne...what was that scent? Sofia retched, but the movement barely registered. "I need one more disappearance to seal the case against Nick, and you're too tempting to pass up. At least you'll get to see your sister again."

*Oh God. Gina.*

Something *thunked* next to her head. Unable to move, her eyelids heavy, she caught the glint of metal. A badge. Another cop. Christmas trees. He smelled like Christmas trees.

Cal.

She whimpered, tried to speak, but her tongue felt two sizes too big for her mouth.

"Shit." The man scooped up the badge, scars turning the skin on the back of his hand into a gnarled mess. "You're going to take a nap now," he said as he checked her pulse and met her watery gaze. "I promise. This won't hurt."

Darkness enveloped her. Something crashed in her living room, then all sounds faded, and she floated for a moment until she disappeared into oblivion.

**Nick**

Emerging from the meeting, Nick fingered the temporary thirty-day chip. It didn't represent his recovery, but at least the feel of it centered him. He turned the coin over in his pocket with one hand as he dialed Sofia with the other.

He'd not meant to go so long without talking to her. Her voicemail answered, and worry strained Nick's tone. "Sofia, love. I just got out of a meeting and I'm headed back to your apartment now. With traffic...I'll probably be half an hour. Text me when you get this."

Nick hung up before the words lingering on his lips could escape. "I love you," he said to the air.

By the time he reached the freeway exit, Nick had gone from worried to panicked. Sofia hadn't called, and though he'd rung her twice more, she hadn't answered. Taking the stairs to her apartment two at a time, his heart leapt into his throat as he spied her door cracked open.

"Sofia!" Nick yelled.

*Fuck. How could he be so stupid?*

As the door swung wide, his desperation rose. "Sofia!" Only silence greeted him. Chow mein noodles littered the floor, spilling out of a grease-stained bag at the entrance to her kitchen. Nick raced through the small apartment, even sweeping open the shower curtain, before returning to her living room. The couch cushions were awry, the lamp next to the couch on its side. He pulled out his phone and dialed 911.

"Boston 911, what's your emergency?" the operator asked.

"Freeze! Hands up, Fairhaven." Two police officers stood in Sofia's doorway, guns drawn. Shock stilled Nick's tongue as the officers approached. "Drop the phone and put your hands behind your head."

"What the fuck are you doing?" As he obeyed their orders, Nick's gaze followed his phone to the ground, his only tether to sanity...to Sofia. "My girlfriend is missing. I was calling 911."

The larger of the two officers grabbed Nick's arm and turned him towards the far wall. "Sofia Oliviera? You're reporting her missing? That's a good one. You're under arrest for suspicion of kidnapping, assault, and human trafficking of Emily Norse, Gina Oliviera, and Sofia Oliviera."

*No. Not Sofia.*

Nick whirled around, his heart seizing as ice filled his veins. He wanted to run, to track down Victor and pummel the man within an inch of his life until he revealed where he'd taken Sofia, but the officer drove his shoulder into Nick's gut, sending him sprawling on his back next to the couch. Before Nick could catch his breath, the cop flipped him over, grabbed his wrist, and twisted his arm behind his back. Tongues of pain licked up his shoulder. A booted foot pressed to his back, and the injuries Mario had inflicted the previous day flared, making it hard for him to breathe.

"You can add resisting arrest, too. You're in deep shit, asshole."

Nick slumped in the officer's hold as they cuffed him and read him his rights, and once they pulled him to his feet, he clenched his jaw hard enough to crack a molar. Not that it mattered. His life was over if he couldn't save Sofia. Nick only had one hope now: stay quiet until he could call Ben. And pray for some sort of miracle.

# 21

## Sofia

TINY CRACKS of light permeated her haze. Sounds rumbled underneath her—all around her. Her body bounced on something hard and pain sliced through her wrists. She couldn't move her arms. Her breath escaped in ragged pants, and she tried to scream, but a thick piece of cloth between her teeth muffled the sound. Kicking, her legs moved as one, her ankles bound tightly.

*Calm down. You're not going to get out of this by panicking.*

Self-talk didn't help her, and she tugged violently against the plastic tie around her wrists until she broke the skin. Whimpering from the pain, and with the scent of blood and exhaust in her nose, the dark space spun around her.

*Focus!*

The pain. She could use the pain. Her hands rested against her ass, and she scraped her fingers against her yoga pants, aggravating the burn from Nick's punishment. Sparks of fire raced up her arms from the cuts around her wrists, and she imagined she was in Nick's bedroom, her arms and legs bound with *his* ropes, his commanding voice in her ear.

*"Get moving, love. Find a way out."*

*"Yes, Sir."*

Trunks had quick-release catches. She said a little prayer of thanks for all those cop shows Gina made her watch over the years. The momentary thought of her sister brought tears to her eyes, but she shook her head, scraping her cheek against a tire iron and wincing.

*"Arms in front of you. You can do this."*

Wriggling as best she could, she tried to maneuver her hands under her ass. The plastic ties bit deeper into her skin. She cried out as she arched her back, stretched her shoulders until she feared they'd pop out of their sockets, and managed to get her arms underneath her.

The gag made it hard to breathe. She choked on the scent of her own blood as she twisted her wrists and struggled to undo the knot behind her head. Spitting the filthy cloth from her mouth, she sucked in air tainted by exhaust and coughed. Next, she had to find a way to get her arms and legs free.

Pushing against the bottom of the trunk, she yelped as the car went over another bump. But her fingers found the tire iron. Leverage. Sofia wedged the tire iron between her legs, pushing and pulling until she thought she might be in the right position. At least these ties were around her thick wool socks.

Gritting her teeth, she twisted the tire iron as she wrenched her legs in the opposite direction. Her head throbbed from the drugs and the fumes, but she couldn't give up. With a last burst of strength, she jerked the tire iron, and the zip tie snapped in two.

Her arms proved more difficult. With so little room to move, she couldn't find a good position, and all she managed to do was deepen the welts around her wrists.

*"Sir, this isn't working."* She needed Nick. Why hadn't she texted him to confirm the lunch order? *Because that's just something he'd do.* Memories swam in and out of focus in her addled

mind. Onions. Christmas trees. *Oh God. The man who took me knows Nick.* What was his name? Charlie? Carl. No. Cal.

Sofia pulled and twisted as hard as she could as she tried to recall Nick's description of Cal. The man who'd delivered the food. He'd worn a hat, but she'd seen the white hair peeking out from under the brim. What had he said to her? He was sorry. He needed Nick in jail. With a sob and one last tug on her bound hands, the plastic snapped, and she fell back, hitting her head on the spare tire.

*"Find a way out of the trunk."*

Imaginary Nick in her head kept her focused. The strips of light around the trunk dimmed, and the sound of traffic became louder, but also muffled. Darkness overtook her, and she started to shake. *Fight.* She could do this. The dark wouldn't kill her, but wherever Cal was taking her, there were certainly people who would. And maybe...Gina. Thoughts of her sister spilled fat tears onto her cheeks, and as the salt mixed with the scrape on her cheek, the sting brought her back to the present. She wriggled forward, hands out, searching for the edges of the trunk. There. Rubber, then metal met her fingertips.

*Keep going. It's a lever or a handle.*

Something sharp sliced into her palm, but she didn't let the injury stop her. Slowly, carefully, she explored her moving prison until her fingers closed around a wide piece of plastic. As the car emerged from the tunnel, the plastic in her hand glowed. He'd have to slow down at some point. Traffic lights, stop signs. How long had she been out? Were they still in Boston? They were traveling at highway speeds. They had to be well outside of the city by now.

It had been sunny when she'd opened her apartment door. But now, what little light seeped into the trunk looked more like twilight than daytime. Sofia fought to stay awake. Between the motion of the car, the fumes, the aftereffects of the drugs, and her injuries, she feared once the car did slow, she'd be too weak to run.

"*I love your strength, kitten.*"

He sounded like he was right next to her. Shit. She was hallucinating now. "Wake the fuck up," she told herself, then grabbed one of her injured wrists. The pain snapped her out of her fog, slicking her fingers with blood. *Stay focused.*

Another bump and then the car turned, sending her careening to one corner of the trunk. She almost lost her grip on the tire iron, but then the car slowed. Sofia scrambled for the quick-release lever. If she hurried, as soon as he stopped, she could get out before he unbuckled his seat belt.

A bubble of laughter escaped on a snort. Who said he was wearing one? He obviously didn't care about the law if he'd drugged her, tied her up, and thrown her in the trunk of his car.

The car jerked to a stop, the brake lights bathing the trunk in an eerie red glow.

Sofia tugged on the lever, and the trunk popped open just an inch. She caught the edge just before the lid started to rise on its own, and peered out into the semi-darkness. Seeing no one, she grasped the tire iron and squeezed out of the narrow opening, falling to the ground and barely managing to stop her weapon from clanging on the asphalt. The car jerked into gear, and she tried to close the trunk, but as her captor hit the gas, her bloody fingers slipped off the edge. Salty, dank air surrounded her, and a ship's horn blared in the distance.

She was out of time. Getting to her feet, she ran in a half-crouch, hoping she'd make it to a large stack of shipping containers to her left before Cal knew she'd escaped. Some sort of dockyard? But where?

Once she reached the corner, she straightened, pumping her legs as she turned down what might as well have been a maze. In the dim light of dusk, the containers took on varying shades of gray, a metallic prison if she couldn't find a way out. Which way? Tires squealed.

Her captor knew she was gone. With a glance to the heavens, hoping somewhere, someone was looking out for her, Sofia turned the direction she thought held the outer edge of whatever shipyard they were in.

Her lungs burned. Every few steps her vision shimmered as a wave of dizziness swamped her. But Sofia kept running.

Shouts echoed off the containers.

"Where is she?"

"How could you be so stupid, Pritchard?"

"She was tied up!" Cal's voice, desperate, didn't sound very far away.

Skidding around another stack of containers, Sofia almost cried out in relief. A large building loomed, no lights glowing in the windows high on the walls. At the far end, perhaps three hundred feet away, stood a pay phone.

But who would she call? Cal had kidnapped her to send Nick to jail. She couldn't call the police. Any of them could be in on it. *"Forlano just sat there sipping his espresso while his enforcer broke my wrist. On the other side of the wall, Damian's Trattoria had a line out the door."*

Nick's words came back to her. Forlano. She could call him. Damian's Trattoria. Would he actually be there?

With one last scan of the area from her hiding spot, Sofia took off at a run. Reaching the phone, she tucked the receiver in the crook of her neck, jabbing the 0 with one hand and holding the tire iron in the other.

"Operator."

"I need to make a collect call. Damian's Trattoria in Boston. This is...Emily Norse. It's urgent. Please hurry."

Using the missing girl's name had the desired effect. The man who picked up the phone accepted the charges. "Emily? Hang on. Boss? Get over here!"

"I don't have much time," Sofia said, keeping her voice a hoarse whisper. "Don't put the phone down. I'm...shit. I'm not Emily, but they took me too. I'm—"

"Who is this?" A different voice, the accent thicker, the tone impatient, boomed over the line.

"I'm Nick Fairhaven's girlfriend. I'm...I don't know where I am. Nick...I think they've arrested him." Two men burst around the far side of the building, and Sofia's heart stopped. "There are shipping containers, I smell the ocean, and this pay phone number is 973-55—shit."

She dropped the phone as the first man barreled towards her. She swung the tire iron wildly. Catching him in the hip, she cried out as the impact sailed up her arms and staggered back, her foot landing on a piece of glass. As the shard dug deep into her skin, she teetered and fell as if in slow motion, her weapon clattering just out of her reach. The second man hauled her up by her arms as she screamed.

"Shut the fuck up, bitch," he growled as he slammed her into the wall. Clamping a hand over her mouth, he pressed his entire body to hers, and she could only watch, helpless, as the man she'd hit limped over to her with a syringe in his hand.

"Night-night," he said as he jabbed the needle into her neck and the world turned soft and cold and dark once more.

"Sof. Please. Wake up." Someone shook her. "Sof?"

Blinking against the dizziness, Sofia tried to make sense of the world around her. A yellow light overhead illuminated the room, which smelled of sweat and fear. The heart-shaped face above her shimmered in and out of focus, drawn, pale, but still so familiar. "Gina?"

"Sof. I'm so sorry..." Her sister sniffled and slid her arm around Sofia's shoulders to help her sit up. "I...should have listened to you. Rick...his name wasn't Rick. We went out clubbing on Friday and...I woke up here!"

Sofia tried to focus on her sister's tear-stained face. With a half-smile, she squeezed Gina's hand. "It's okay, baby girl."

"It's not!" Gina wailed. "They're going to...*sell* us!"

"No. Not...if I can help it." Sofia shook her head, and nausea flooded her. "Oh God. I'm going to be sick."

"Here." Gina pressed a bottle to Sofia's lips. Stale, cloudy water had never tasted so good. "Whatever they gave all of us...it wears off pretty quick, but don't move around yet. Otherwise, you'll hurl."

"All of us?" Blinking hard, Sofia took in her surroundings. They were in some sort of long, narrow room with a toilet and sink in one corner and a door on the opposite wall. A few feet away, five other women huddled, dressed in skimpy club-appropriate attire, wearing identical expressions of fear and exhaustion. Tear-stained cheeks, stringy hair, barefoot, and curled together as if safety resided in numbers.

"Do you have any idea where we are? I mean...physically?"

"I think we're somewhere in Jersey. Becca said she smelled Jersey as they took her out of the van," Gina said. "But...the rest of us woke up here."

Had she stayed on the phone long enough? Could Damian Forlano figure out where they were? Though, for all she knew, they could be miles from the pay phone.

*Nick, I'm sorry.*

Unable to hold her head up any longer, Sofia rested her cheek against Gina's shoulder. She'd been so stupid. She should have confronted Gina about the drugs before her interview. Maybe then her baby sister would have been able to get away. "I found a baggie under the couch," she murmured, whatever they'd used to subdue her causing her words to slur and her eyelids to droop. "Rick's?"

Her sister shuddered. "Yeah. I blew it off. Told myself as long as he wasn't asking me to get high with him, I could still have fun. He's an asshole," Gina said as she swiped a hand over her tear-stained cheek. "Pretty sure his real name is Anton. He works with that guy from your club."

Sliding her arm around her sister's waist, Sofia winced as Gina's sequined top grazed the abrasions around her wrist. "We have to get out of here," Sofia said softly as another wave of nausea roiled in her stomach.

"They have guns, Sof. And they took our shoes. Lauren, Emily, and Stephanie have been here more than a week. Becca came last night. We only get a couple of granola bars a day. They don't want us strong enough to fight."

Sofia straightened, rubbed her temples, and took a good look at her sister. Gina's eyes were hollow, her cheeks sunken and dirty. A tear in her miniskirt revealed a deep bruise on her thigh.

"How many of them are there?" Trying to hold on to the hope that had burned so brightly when she'd spied the payphone, Sofia cradled one injured wrist, relieved to find at least she wasn't bleeding anymore.

Gina's lower lip wobbled. "At least seven. They haven't touched us. We're...more valuable if we're not...damaged." Tears spilled over, and Sofia wrapped her baby sister in her arms and let her cry. "I should have listened to you, Sof. I should have stayed home and watched movies with you and made you break-fast and done all those things you did for me for so many years."

"Shhh, baby girl. We're going to get out of this somehow." Sofia didn't believe her own words, but she had to do...something. Anything.

Gina flinched when the lock *thunked* and the door swung open. The other girls whimpered and scrambled as far from the door as they could. A shadow loomed, one with spiked hair. Sofia let go of Gina and pushed to her feet, swaying a little. "Leo? What the fuck are you doing?"

"Making a shit-ton of money." He stepped forward, the light from the single overhead bulb casting his face and his jagged hairline in dim shadows. He had a gun in one hand, pointed right at her, and a bag in the other. "I'm sorry I had to get you involved, Sofia. But we need your boyfriend to go down for this. And your disappearance just guaranteed he'll never breathe free air again."

## 22

Sofia

ANGER SIMMERED under the surface of her fear, a red-hot prickle that displaced the nausea and dizziness that had been her constant companion since she'd regained consciousness in the trunk of the car. "What did you do to Nick?"

"He's being charged with three counts of kidnapping. Iron-clad evidence. Especially with how much noise you made last night. Your neighbors were only too happy to confirm they heard you screaming several times. Not to mention, the photos."

"Photos?" Sofia took a step forward, but her injured foot sent pain racing up her leg, and she crashed to her hands and knees with a whimper. Leo dropped the bag, bent, and grabbed her chin, forcing her to meet his gaze. "You're very pretty when you're tied up, Sofia. I didn't think you'd have much value as inventory. But you garnered one of the highest bids of this auction. Though the damage you inflicted on yourself...*tsk tsk*."

He shoved her back and reached into his pocket. When he turned the phone around, tears burned Sofia's eyes. She stood in her living room, her arms bound over her head, wearing only her thong. The picture was black and white, a little grainy, but the look on her face...somewhere between joy and pain. "How...?"

"Hidden camera in your ficus." Leo shrugged. "Once you and lover boy started hanging out, I had Anton put up a camera to keep an eye on you. In case you didn't respond to Victor's threats. I'd have been happy seeing that rich bastard drawn into the poker game. That alone would have been enough to cast suspicion on him. Victor would have been occupied with a new whale on the hook, and he'd have stopped obsessing over the missing security footage. But...after last night...I never knew you were so...expressive."

Sofia slapped him. With a grunt, Leo grabbed her by the hair and pulled her to her feet, then slammed her against the wall. Stars exploded in her vision as she whimpered. "Behavior like that won't be tolerated by your new owner." His thin lips curled into a smile. "You're already banged up. What's another bruise?"

His fingers left her hair, but before her knees buckled, he punched her in the jaw. Pain replaced every other sensation, centering just below her left eye and radiating out in endless waves. The door slammed shut as Sofia collapsed into her sister's arms.

Gina sobbed as Sofia tried to breathe through the throbbing agony. With shaking fingers, she touched her cheek.

*Please don't be broken.*

She wasn't sure why she cared. If they didn't get out of there soon, it wouldn't matter. A broken bone would be the least of her problems.

"D-do you know when they're m-moving us?" Sofia asked. "How long do we have?"

"Tomorrow." One of the other girls—Emily—snatched the bag Leo dropped and tore into it. "Only four bars. We'll have to share."

Sofia pushed up on an elbow. "Can they hear us in here? Does anyone know?"

"I don't think so." Gina shook her head. "I screamed a lot the first day."

"Everyone screams their first day," a quiet voice said from the corner. "Except you." The woman's gray gaze met Sofia's. Though she was dirty and looked like she hadn't eaten in a week, fire burned in the depths of her eyes. "You're stronger."

"I got away once," Sofia said as she held up her hands. "Leo's one guy. Yes, one guy with a gun. But unless all seven of them are waiting outside that door, we've got a chance." Struggling to her feet, Sofia limped over to the narrow door. The deadbolt looked solid, and she thought she'd heard a chain rattle before the door had opened. *No one's strong enough to break the door down. Keep looking.*

Heading for the corner with the toilet and sink, Sofia peered up into the darkness near the ceiling. Pipes disappeared into cheap drywall at least fifteen feet up. "Too high to reach," she murmured. Even if they stood on the sink, and she didn't think anyone was steady enough to do that. They'd have to think their way out of this. She nodded towards the bag in Emily's hands. "I don't need food. If we want to get out of here, we need to make sure the weakest eat the most. Because we're going to have to fight. And run."

Back at her sister's side, Sofia sat cross-legged and twined her fingers with Gina's as she swept her gaze over the other girls. "Tell me everything you know about their patterns."

**Nick**

Slamming his hand down on the table in front of him as much as he could with the cuffs locked to a metal hasp in the center of the old, scarred metal top, Nick swore. "Bloody hell, we've been over this five times already!"

"Mr. Fairhaven, if you expect to ever get out of this room, you'll answer our questions."

"You've kept me here for over three hours without my lawyer. I know my rights, Detective. I demand to be allowed to call Ben Hetherington immediately." Nick shoved at the table, and the detective stood with his hand on his weapon. "For fuck's sake. Do you honestly think you're in any danger in this room?" Nick asked, trying not to roll his eyes as he lifted his bound hands. "I'm cuffed to a fucking table."

"Can't be too careful," Detective Sampson said, holding up one finger. "You have a reputation for violence. An altercation at your office two years ago."

"Where a loan shark came after *me*. Not the other way around. I didn't throw a single punch."

The detective cocked his head as he added a second finger. "Ms. Oliviera screamed several times last night—when you were beating her."

"Beating her? I've never—" He shut his mouth. Trying to explain to the detective that Sofia had been screaming in ecstasy would get him nowhere.

"And resisting arrest." A third finger rose, the detective's middle one, and Nick's anger boiled over.

"Let me remind you of the facts, Detective. Your officers manhandled *me* during the arrest, and I have the bruises to prove it. I did not resist. I can demonstrate a consistent pattern of harassment following the night I saved Emily Norse from her assailant at Bound. If you expect to have a career at all when this is over, you'll give me my goddamned phone call."

Detective Sampson puffed out his chest. His lips curved into a knowing smile. "Oh, I don't think I'll be the one who has to worry about a career, Fairhaven. Your choices are going to be limited to the laundry, the prison library, and kitchen duty."

A rap on the glass startled the detective, and he glared at the two-way mirror. Another rap, this one more insistent, and the man almost snarled. "Don't move," he admonished Nick.

"As if I could."

Alone, Nick clenched his hands into fists. They'd taken his watch, along with his wallet, keys, and the one-month chip he ached to have in his hands right now. He only knew the time because he'd glanced at the detective's watch when the man had rolled up his sleeves. Three and a half hours since he'd walked into Sofia's apartment. How long before then had she been taken? An hour? Two? He tried to remember when he'd texted her. Not long after noon.

What was he going to do if he couldn't get her back? If she'd fallen victim to the traffickers—he shook his head as he stopped himself. If? He had no illusions that she was anywhere else. Unless whoever had taken her had killed her.

Nick yanked at the cuffs, knowing he'd get nowhere, but unable to sit still a moment longer. What the hell was he going to do? The longer he sat here, the greater the chance that he'd never see Sofia again.

"Detective!" He jerked his hands again, rocking the table. "I demand to be able to call my lawyer. Right bloody now!"

The door slammed open, and Ben's tall frame filled the doorway. "Nick, don't say another word."

"The hell I won't. They have—"

Ben held up his hand. "I know. Sit there for five more minutes without incriminating yourself and you'll walk out of the station with me. Say another word, and I can't guarantee shit."

Appropriately chastised, Nick flopped back in the chair and tried to slow his heart rate from somewhere approximating Usain Bolt's running cadence. What the hell was going on?

Ben was as good as his word. Not more than five minutes later, Detective Sampson stalked back into the room, murderous rage pinching his rat-like features as he unlocked Nick's cuffs. "If you step a single toe out of line, you're going to be washing prison bedding for the rest of your life."

"Detective, do you have a foot fetish?" Nick bared his teeth in a vague approximation of a smile as he passed the man he'd rather pummel into the ground than ever speak to again.

Ben jabbed Nick in the ribs as the two men headed for the station doors. "You're either living under a charmed star or you've got the worst luck of anyone I've ever met," he whispered.

"The latter." Nick ran a hand through his hair, the reddened flesh at his wrists not even the start of the penance he'd owe if he couldn't save Sofia. "How did you know?"

"Just wait." Ben led Nick down the precinct steps and gestured to an idling Mercedes with tinted windows. "Get in the back."

Ben slid into the passenger seat while Nick flung open the rear door, then stared, slack-jawed, at the man lounging in the back seat.

Damian Forlano angled his head, a grim set to his jaw. "Well, don't just stand there, Nick. Get in. Your Sofia doesn't have a lot of time."

## 23

Nick

DAMIAN HANDED NICK A PHONE. "Play the message." As the car sped away from the precinct, Sofia's voice came over the speaker.

"I'm...I don't know where I am. Nick...I think they've arrested him. There are shipping containers all around me, I smell the ocean, and this pay phone number is 973-55—shit."

As the sounds of a scuffle followed by Sofia's scream filled the car, Nick squeezed the phone hard enough he felt the plastic crack. "Where is she?"

Damian eased the phone from Nick's hand. "My guys tracked that pay phone prefix to the Port Newark Container Terminal in New Jersey. There are a dozen phones over about two hundred acres, but only a quarter of the terminal's deserted enough that no one would have heard her scream."

"Call the New Jersey police—" Anger flared, white-hot, when Damian shook his head. "Why the fuck not?"

"Did you forget where you were a few minutes ago? Also, a 'thank you' is in order." Damian leaned forward and said something to the driver in Italian before turning back to Nick. "Your Sofia is the only reason you're not still stuck in that interrogation room. I can't tell you how many cops Victor has in his back pocket, but you're lucky I have more. Otherwise, you wouldn't have seen your lawyer until at least tomorrow, and the girls would probably be halfway to Minsk."

Nick sank against the rich leather seat. "I can't let her be..." He couldn't say the words, couldn't imagine what they could be doing to her at this very moment. His hands shook as he pulled the one-month coin from his pocket. Ben had retrieved the confiscated items before pulling him out of interrogation. Spinning the coin over one knuckle to the next and then back again, he found a small measure of sanity. "Please, Damian. Help me get her back. She's...I love her."

"A blind man could see that." Damian checked his watch. "We'll be at Norwood Airport in twenty minutes. I have a private plane waiting to take us to New Jersey. Five of my men will join us."

"I want one more." Nick had never felt this alone. Not even the very first day he went to a Gamblers Anonymous meeting. "Cal Pritchard. He's a police lieutenant. A friend."

Damian arched a brow. "Are you willing to bet your life— Sofia's life—on any member of the police force at this moment?"

Nick fixed Damian with a hard stare. "I can count those I trust on one hand right now: Sofia, Alex, Elizabeth, Ben, and Cal. We're crossing state lines, presumably armed, to stop a human trafficking ring. I'd feel a lot better if we had a cop with us."

Damian pressed his hand to his heart. "After bailing you out of jail, I didn't make the list? How very rude. Fine. Call him. But if he can't get to the airport in twenty minutes, we're leaving without him."

It took Nick three tries to dial Cal's number. Every time he tried, he heard Sofia scream and his fingers would slip.

"Nick? Are you okay?" Cal's raspy voice crackled over the poor connection. "Where are you?"

"How quickly can you get to Norwood Airport?"

"I'm in New York City with Hannah. Her mother invited us up for dinner." Muffled words Nick couldn't understand carried over the line before Cal's voice cleared again. "Why?"

"Cal, I hate to ask. But can you meet us in Jersey...at—" Nick glanced at Damian, angling the phone so Cal could hear Damian's response.

"Teterboro. We'll be there at 10:15 p.m."

Cal coughed. "New Jersey? What the hell are you doing going to New Jersey? You're a suspect in multiple kidnappings, Nick. Leaving the state...hell, even leaving the city is a huge fucking risk."

"Victor has Sofia. We might have an idea where she is, but... shite, Cal. I won't let her be...sold." Nick forced the last word over the lump in his throat. "Please."

"I'll be there. Don't leave the airport without me."

When Nick disconnected the call, Ben turned in his seat to stare at Damian. "Are you sure about this? Where they are?"

"You think the mob is all about breaking bones?" Damian leaned forward, eyes narrowed. "This is the twenty-first century, Benjamin. I have a network of computer experts I can call upon at a moment's notice. There are two-dozen private warehouses at the terminal. Three of them are owned by shell corporations my people can't trace. Four others have been rented in the past several months to private individuals."

"So?" Ben asked.

Nick's mind reeled. "Shite." Glancing from Damian to Ben, he explained. "The Port of Newark is one of the largest shipping ports in the world. More than forty percent of Fairhaven Exports' shipments enter the United States at the ports of New York and New Jersey. Private citizens don't own—or lease—warehouses.

Not unless they're planning something untoward. And very, very lucrative."

"And the shell corporations?" Ben asked.

Damian rubbed his chin, his fingers rasping against a layer of stubble. "They could be legitimate. However, two of them were formed less than a month ago."

Nick's phone buzzed in his hand. "Alex?"

"I hope you know what you're doing." Alexander's weary voice held no judgment, only concern. "Ben told me what happened. I'm sorry, Nicholas. I should have done more...sooner. My FBI contact believes that there's a *shipment* of women"—Alex's tone carried more venom than Nick had ever heard—"leaving the United States for Russia tomorrow afternoon from somewhere on the East Coast. But he doesn't know where they are now, whether they're traveling by plane or boat, or who is behind it all."

The car jerked to a halt outside a private terminal and Nick glanced out the window. A small Gulf Stream idled, engines running. "New Jersey," Nick said as he threw open the car door. "We're heading there now."

"We?" Alex asked. His voice dropped. "I'll be right back, *chérie*." Footsteps echoed over the line. "These people are killers, Nicholas."

"You ran after a hitman to protect Elizabeth. They have Sofia, and it's all my fault. I love her, Alex." Damian gestured for Nick to hurry up and board the plane. "When this is over, I hope you'll have a chance to meet her."

"As do I."

Nick ran a hand through his hair. How did you tell your brother you might be flying to your death? With a sigh, he climbed the steps to the Gulf Stream. "Take care of Elizabeth, Alex. And yourself. I love you."

The forty-five-minute flight to Teterboro felt like an eternity. Mario spread a map of the shipyard out on a small conference table once they'd reached cruising height. "The most likely building is this one," he said as he circled a large, square structure in the north-east corner of the yard. "There's a pay phone with the same prefix Sofia gave us five hundred feet away."

Damian glanced around the small group of his men, all with pistols secured at their hips or in chest harnesses. "We split up. My cousin is sending an additional five men. We will be twelve."

"Thirteen," Nick said. "Cal will meet us there." He rubbed the back of his neck. Only two buildings away from the port exit. She'd been so close to freedom. "That building is mine," he said, trying to force some strength into his voice. "I don't care what the rest of you do. Cal and I are hitting that one."

"You're not going anywhere without me, Nick," Damian said. "I paid your bail. If you die, I'm out a very large sum of money."

"Fine. Are you going to trust me with a gun?"

Mario chuckled. "You know how to use one, *stronzo*?"

"I was in the Royal Navy for three years. Yes, I know how to use a gun." Nick straightened to his full height, which still left him three inches shorter than Mario. But something in his tone must have conveyed his determination, because the man grunted what might have been an acknowledgment and retrieved a belt holster and a Glock for Nick, along with a switchblade.

"Don't shoot yourself."

"I don't *want* to shoot anyone. Except perhaps Victor. Or anyone who put their hands on Sofia."

The pilot announced their descent. Nick dropped into a chair and secured his seatbelt. *Sofia, I'm coming for you, love. Hang on a little longer.*

Nick's phone buzzed with a voicemail message from Cal as soon as he turned it back on. He and Damian slid into the back seat of a nondescript black sedan while Mario took the wheel. "Cal's going to meet us at the port in fifteen minutes."

"Then we'd better hurry. Mario?" Damian buckled his seat-belt as his enforcer slammed his foot down on the gas.

By the time they reached the outer gates of the port, it was past midnight. Nick fingered the switchblade Damian had given him. Despite the reassuring presence of the gun at his hip, the blade held more appeal. He'd always been better at close-quar-ters fighting. In the Royal Navy, he'd excelled at hand-to-hand, though he'd not used those skills in years.

Cal waited, parked a hundred feet away from the locked gates. As he jogged over to the other twelve men, he kept his gaze fixed on Nick. "Listen, if you kill any of these assholes who took your girl, I can't protect you."

With a glare, Damian snorted. "You couldn't protect your friend here from a sloppy police investigation. Do you really think I'd trust you to protect *me* from anything?"

Nick slapped a hand on each of the men's chests. "Shut it. Both of you. Sofia's in there somewhere about to be *sold*. I'm going in to get her. There's every chance I'm going to die without your help."

Muttering a few choice curse words, Mario took a large pair of bolt cutters and snapped the heavy chain that locked the port gate. "You're all going to die if we don't get a move on."

"You heard Mario," Nick said, which earned him a chuckle from the man he thought hated him. They rushed through the gate and Mario led the way towards the pay phone Sofia had used.

When they reached the corner of the warehouse, Mario pointed a small flashlight at the phone. Blood smeared the o key and the receiver, and Nick's heart seized.

"Over there," Damian whispered, his penlight aimed at the corner of the building.

Silver glinted. Sofia's bracelet lay next to bloody glass shard. Nick snatched the delicate chain from the ground and held it to his heart. "She was here. Where do we go next?"

"We split up," Mario said as he ran back from the next building. "There's a blood trail leading to the north-east, but it ends just before that door."

"And skid marks this way," one of the New Jersey men said as he gestured in the opposite direction.

Damian extended his arms and Nick, Mario, and three of his men huddled in close. "I am going with Nick and his cop friend. Mario, go with Pietro and Sammy. Once you clear the second building, join us. All phones on silent. You find anything, you call three times in a row. Otherwise, no contact. No distractions." He dropped his voice so Cal couldn't hear. "You kill anyone who gets in your way, but if you see that *testa di cazzo* in charge, you leave him alive. For me."

They broke the huddle and Nick unsnapped the piece of leather that held his gun in the holster. What he wouldn't give to have Milos at his side right now. Or any of Alex's men. But Damian's enforcers were virtually above the law—or well below it. While Nick didn't trust them any further than he could throw them, they wanted Emily back almost as much as he wanted to have Sofia in his arms again.

"*Buona fortuna uomini*," Damian said and he, Cal, and Nick ducked their heads and took off at a run.

## Sofia

Gina dozed against her, the soft snores Sofia had always hated now the most welcome sound in the world. They'd all agreed to sleep in shifts in case Leo or one of his men opened the door and there was any chance of escape. Sofia had torn strips from her yoga pants to tie around her injured foot, but she couldn't do anything about the swelling under her left eye. Her head throbbed, both from hunger and the punch, but after several hours of talking, she'd convinced the girls to try to fight.

With a gasp, Gina sat up. "Shit," she whispered as she glanced around the small room. "I thought...maybe..."

"I know, baby girl." Sofia smoothed Gina's hair, the unruly locks tangled by too many days spent in this hell hole. "We're going to get out of this."

Gina shifted, meeting Sofia's gaze in the dim light. "You know I hate it when you call me that, right?"

"Baby girl? Yeah. But..."

"It was Mom's nickname for me." Swiping at a tear that tumbled down her cheek, Gina hunched her shoulders. "It made me feel safe after they died. But then...I dunno. Sometime in college, it started to feel patronizing."

Sofia took her sister's hands. "I'm sorry. Look, I know I haven't been the greatest...mom. I wasn't ready. But—"

With a sob, Gina threw her arms around her sister. "I love you, Sof. You were the best mom. Well, other than Mom. I just...I wanted a *sister*."

The two held on to one another until neither had any more tears to cry, then Gina went to the sink and refilled a dirty water bottle. Handing it to Sofia, she chewed on her lip for a minute. "If we don't get out of this...if we don't end up...together..."

"Stop that right now," Sofia said sharply. "We're going to—"

The chain on the door clanked and all of the girls tensed.

Sofia and Gina crouched against the wall with Emily cowering in front of them as cover. Lauren and Stephanie pressed themselves against the corners of the room while Becca hid behind the door. Trying to ignore the pain in her foot—and her head—Sofia prayed maybe...just maybe...her plan might work.

## 24

Sofia

THE DOOR OPENED SLOWLY, and one of the men who'd captured Sofia by the pay phone entered with his gun leveled at the women at the back of the room. "Boss says it's time to go. You in the back first." He glared at Sofia and Gina. "You're last. Either of you move, and I'll give you a nice parting gift." The man jerked his belt as he thrust his hips at them, and Gina spat on his shoes.

"We're worth more untouched, you piece of shit. I bet ol' Leo wouldn't be very happy with you 'damaging the merchandise.'"

The thug clocked Emily on the head with the butt of his gun. She whimpered as she threw her hands up to protect herself and curled into the fetal position.

With a quick glance at the other women, Sofia nodded. Piercing cries echoed off the walls as every single woman started to scream and Becca shoved the door at the man with the gun. The momentary distraction worked, and the gunman stumbled back.

Sofia and Gina rushed the man, Sofia grabbing his gun hand and Gina kneeing him in the groin. Though she'd tried for his weak point—his wrist—she only managed to swing his arm towards the ceiling, the gun still gripped firmly in his thick fingers. He shoved her back, and she landed only a foot from the door.

The other girls pushed to their feet, some quickly, others wavering as they tried to find their footing after so long half-starved in a small, dark room. "Go," Becca hissed.

With one last look back at the others, all terrified, but now willing to fight and advancing on the thug with the gun, Sofia grabbed Gina's hand.

*Now or never.* Hell, this had been Sofia's plan. Why did she suddenly hate it? Because she had no guarantee the other girls would get out. But everyone had agreed. Sofia and Gina were the strongest.

"Race you to the outside," Gina said as she burst through the door and pulled her sister into a brightly lit warehouse space. Temporarily blinded, Sofia stumbled, but Gina's iron grip on her hand kept her going.

"You'd...win," Sofia panted as they reached the edge of the room. "Ms. High School...track star."

"Which way?" Gina whispered as she yanked open a door to a long hallway.

"I don't know." Sofia took a single breath, all of her prayers focused on the answer. "Left?" Not that she knew why. Gina's bare feet made sharp slapping noises on the concrete floors, and every step sent shooting pains up Sofia's leg from her injured foot.

"Hey, at least you have socks."

Sofia spared her sister a single glance, catching the hint of a smile. They'd do this. They'd escape. The Oliviera girls had never given up before. Not when their parents had died. Not when they'd been evicted from their first apartment. Not now.

Around a corner and into another hallway, Sofia cursed the maze. Empty offices broken up by short stretches of hallways, supply closets, and ladders to a second floor where along one side of the building, storage crates were stacked twenty-high.

"In here," Sofia said, pulling Gina into an office with a door that led presumably to the other side of the building. Her head swam, the lights hurting her eyes and making the walls spin around them every few steps.

"Stop right now, bitches!" Leo's angry voice pierced the quiet room, and a bullet whizzed over Sofia's shoulder. She and Gina dropped to a crouch behind a large desk. "There's no way out of this building. Run around all you want. My men are everywhere."

Though fear and adrenaline churned in Sofia's empty stomach, she tugged Gina towards the far door. "We have to keep going."

They sprinted for the exit, and Sofia's fingers brushed against the knob as Leo tackled her. The two crashed into the door, and Sofia's head hit the wall. A bright light obscured her vision, and blood dribbled down her neck, hot and sticky.

Leo grabbed her wrist, flipping her over and twisting her arm behind her back. Sofia screamed as her shoulder threatened to pop out of its socket.

*No. We were so close...*

Though she tried to keep fighting, to scissor her legs and buck her body to throw Leo off of her, he was twice her weight. When he captured her other wrist, she screamed again as the scabs from the zip ties broke open and Leo pulled a fresh plastic cuff from his pocket.

"No!" she cried just as a high-pitched scream came from behind her. Leo's weight shifted, freeing her left wrist from his iron grip. Sofia kicked and wriggled free, then stared in horror as her baby sister wrapped her arms around Leo's neck and tried to cut off his airway.

"Go," Gina panted. "Run. I got this."

"Not without you!" Her head hurt. Two Ginas grappled with two Leos until she blinked hard. Sofia grabbed a chair and swung it at Leo, but the man jumped at the last minute, then backed into a wall, sending the air *whooshing* from Gina's lungs.

"Go," Gina grunted.

As Sofia turned, she heard her sister whimper. *Don't look back. Keep going. Find help. Or...*

Leo cursed, his voice strained. Sofia almost turned, but after another shot rang out, she pushed forward.

Run. She had to run.

**Nick**

Nick, Cal, and Damian approached a large room, Cal in the lead with his gun drawn. The space was littered with coffee cups and old hamburger wrappers.

"Sunday 0800. The Royal Gale," Cal read off a whiteboard on the wall.

"This is the right place," Damian spat. "That ship's headed for Vladivostok tomorrow." At Nick's shocked look, he continued with a shrug. "I studied the shipping manifests on the way to bail you out of jail."

Nick's respect for the brutish Italian rose a notch. For all of his Old World mafioso tendencies, the man had a head for business. If Nick still ran Fairhaven Exports, he'd look for someone with Damian's analysis skills to work for him.

The three headed for another door at the far end of the room, but steps away, Nick's heart stopped as a woman screamed. He couldn't tell through the walls and the echoing hallways if the scream had come from Sofia, but if he found one of the women, maybe he'd find all of them. Including the one he loved.

Without a word to the others, he turned on his heel and raced back out the door. Nothing else mattered. Not Damian. Not Cal. Not any friend or foe he might encounter. He had to find Sofia.

The place was a fucking maze. He pulled the gun from its holster, flicking off the safety as he raced down the hall. At a corner, he skidded to a stop and held his breath to listen. No one close. But had he heard a door?

Angling a quick gaze around the corner, he took off again. Should he risk calling out? No. If he did that, he could bring Victor and his men down right on top of him. Or her.

Halfway down a central corridor, his foot slipped, nearly sending him crashing into a wall. Glancing down at the crimson smudge, he could only see the piece of bloody glass next to the phone booth. The trail stopped next to a narrow door, and as he pressed his ear to the wood, he thought he heard ragged breathing.

*Please.*

Nick aimed the gun, trying to keep his hand from shaking as he yanked open the door. The woman cowering in the corner of the supply closet brandishing a mop bore little resemblance to his Sofia. Dirty, bloody, and with a feral, desperate look in her eyes, she swung the mop as she sprang forward.

"Sofia! Stop. It's Nick." He caught her around the waist and pulled her against him. She struggled, sobbing, until he shoved the gun back into its holster and lifted her, carrying her deep into the closet and pulling the door closed behind them. "Look at me, love. Please."

Wild, unfocused eyes scanned his face—or tried—through a purple swelling from her cheek to her temple. "N-Nick?" Sagging in his arms, she lost all fight as he smoothed a hand over her hair.

"I've got you. Deep breaths now. He sank down onto a crate with her in his lap. "How badly are you hurt?"

"I...don't know. Gina...she's—"

A shot reverberated through the warehouse and Nick and

Sofia flinched. He reached for his gun again, but she clung to his arms, her words tumbling out in a rush.

"I lost Gina. She tried to stop Leo...fought him so I could get away...get help. We have to find her. They're moving the rest of the girls. To the ship. Wasn't supposed to be until tomorrow. I'm sorry...God. I'm so sorry. I shouldn't have opened the door. But he said you'd sent food. And that sounded like you. He knew. He knew you. Knew you'd be at a meeting. Knew I'd be alone. I made it so easy. For him to take me." Her voice faded into hiccupping sobs.

"What are you talking about, love? Who took you?" Nick's gut churned. Anguish washed over the bruises and cuts on her face as she tried to wipe away her tears. He caught her hand, the deep, bloody welts around her wrists setting off a storm of anger inside him. "Who. Did. This."

Sofia deflated under his stare and tried twice to form words before Nick cupped her uninjured cheek. "Tell me, love."

"His arm," she said on a gasp. "Burn scars." Nick's hand fell away, and she tried to reach for his fingers, but he pulled back. "H-he smelled like...onions...and Christmas trees."

The room around him spun and tilted. He shifted Sofia out of his arms, and though she tried to cling to him, she lacked the strength to fight as he started to pace.

"I'm so sorry. I should have fought harder, done...something... more," she sobbed as she curled into a ball next to the crates.

Nick dipped his hand in his pocket, withdrawing the one-month chip. "No. Not Cal."

"He...didn't tell me his name," she whispered. "But...yes."

"What did he look like?" Nick knelt next to her, his fingers tight on her arms. Too tight, he realized as tears spilled down her swollen and stained cheeks. "Shite. Sofia, I'm sorry." He smoothed his hands over the old cardigan. "Tell me, love. Please."

"Salt and pepper hair. One...crooked tooth." With every word, a piece of Nick's world crumbled into dust. Meeting Cal at his first Gamblers Anonymous meeting. All of the middle-of-the-night phone calls when the urge to get roaring drunk and call his bookie reared—so powerful, there were days he couldn't be alone. Nights he'd spent in Cal's guest room, reading stories to Cal's children, Hannah teaching him to cook. Cal meeting him here. Visiting his in-laws? The girls moved twelve hours early. After Nick had called Cal.

"Black sedan. A dent...in the right...fender."

Her voice faded as she wrapped her arms around her knees and dropped her head. "He said...he was sorry."

A volley of gunfire sounded. The other side of the warehouse —or so Nick hoped. He focused on Sofia. The woman he loved. Cowering. Ashamed. Hunted.

The chip clattered to the floor.

"Sofia, look at me, love." Nick gathered her into his arms as she cried silently. "Cal's here. I brought him with me. If we're going to get out of here, we have to hurry."

## 25

Nick

SOFIA LOOKED UP AT HIM, her red-rimmed eyes filled with tears. "You and...Cal...alone?"

"No. Damian's here. Along with a lot of his men. Ten of them. They're all armed. We just have to find them." Nick wrapped his arms around Sofia's waist and lifted her to her feet. Shite. Her entire body trembled, and as she tried to put weight on her left foot, she stifled a cry.

"Sit. Let me look at that." Nick peeled off Sofia's sock, wincing at the deep, bloody gash. "We have to stop the bleeding."

"S'why I...hid in here," she said, her first semi-calm sentence since he'd found her. "Also...dizzy."

Nick glanced around the room. The old bulb bathed the supplies in a yellowish glow. He found a folded pile of what he hoped were clean rags on a high shelf. Tearing two of the rags into long strips, he used several as a pad to absorb the blood and more to tie the bandage around her foot.

He held her foot for a long breath as he scanned her face. Her toes were so cold. "How...how badly are you hurt?" The one question he wanted to ask, he couldn't, but Sofia understood.

"They didn't touch me...like that. We were...*worth more* if we were..." She shook her head, pressing her shaking fingers to her swollen temple. "My head is killing me. I can walk. Maybe run. Just," her voice cracked, "don't leave me."

Nick pulled Sofia into his arms. "I'll never leave you again, love. I promise. Let's get out of here, yeah?" Digging into his pocket, Nick withdrew the switchblade Damian had given him. "Take this. We'll head back to where I left Damian and Cal." At her shudder, Nick made a soft shushing sound. "Damian's armed. And the meanest tosser you'll ever meet when he's pissed. Do you know how many men Victor has?"

"Not Victor," she said as Nick stopped and pressed his ear to the door. "Leo. The bar manager. I don't think Victor knows anything about this. The poker game...distracts him from...what Leo's doing." Her words were a little slurred, but as he spared her a quick glance, relief infused his limbs. Sofia's eyes had cleared slightly, and even with the bruises and the bloody gash on her cheek, she was the most beautiful woman he'd ever seen.

At his pause, her brows furrowed. He leaned down to cup the back of her neck and press a kiss to the little wrinkle. "I thought I'd lost you."

"I thought you had too."

Nick cracked the door, gun drawn, and glanced up and down the hall. "We're clear. Left down the hall, take a right, then at the end of that corridor there's a big room—tables and chairs. From there, it's just a couple more turns to get outside."

She nodded gingerly, lacing her fingers through his free hand. "The ship..."

"Forlano knows the name of it. He already called the port authorities. Come on. Let's go."

Though her limp worsened every few steps, they jogged back in the direction Nick had come. Pain twisted her lips, but she kept pace with him, her breathing ragged. When they reached the large room, Nick swore. Blood was splattered on the wall, several of the chairs had been overturned, and a large pool of crimson marred with shoe prints spread out below the spatter.

"Fuck. We're getting out of here," he whispered. "Outside. We have to find Damian. And his men."

Shouts and gunfire—not close, thank God—made Sofia yelp, and Nick tugged her back out the door. She stumbled, continuing to glance behind them as he swept her up into his arms. "Hold on, love. The exit's not far."

Around another corner—just how many goddamned hallways were in this fucking place?—Sofia screamed and tried to launch herself from his arms, taking him down with her as a loud *crack* reverberated within the narrow space. Pain lanced Nick's hip, an all-consuming fire that seemed to spread down his leg and up his back. The two of them landed in a tangle of limbs, the gun tumbling from Nick's grasp.

"Don't move," Cal ordered as his footsteps thundered up behind them. He grabbed Sofia by the arm, hauling her against his body and pressing the gun to her cheek. "You've been a lot of fucking trouble."

She struggled against his hold, but he'd pinned her arms, and he jabbed the gun harder against the already-purple swelling under her eye. "Please...just let us go," Sofia whimpered.

Through the agony, Nick tried to get his left leg under him but failed, the blood soaking into his pants as he hit the ground again. "Cal—"

"Not another word, Nick. On your knees. Face the wall. Your girlfriend's coming with me. You...well, I came around the corner and found you beating the crap out of her. I shouted for you to stop, but you didn't. So I had to shoot you. Too bad one of your partners grabbed Sofia and took off with her before I could get off another shot."

Sofia thrashed, screaming, "I'm not going *anywhere* with—"

Cal slammed the gun against the side of Sofia's head, and she slumped forward. He lowered her to the ground just behind him, too far away for Nick to get to her. If he could even stand.

A fresh wave of betrayal swamped him. "We were friends..."

Cal frowned, a deep sadness ghosting his features. "There are no friends at the bottom. Only marks. Targets. People you can use. You know that, Nick. I...got in too deep. Couldn't stop myself. Leo gave me one chance to get square. Help him, and he'd wipe my debt away. Get him another girl. Set you up to take the fall. It's you or me. I'm...sorry." Regret swam in Cal's bloodshot and watery eyes. He raised the gun and cocked the hammer.

Nick squeezed his eyes shut, preparing for the shot, for the pain, for death...but instead, he heard only the snap of the switchblade, followed by Cal's anguished scream.

Blood spread out around Cal's right foot and soaked into his pants. With both hands gripping the switchblade, Sofia thrust the knife deeper into the cop's leg. She twisted the blade, and Cal stumbled forward, swinging his gun arm towards Sofia.

"No!" Nick grunted as he pushed himself to his feet, ignoring the dark spots floating in his vision. Lunging for Cal, he knocked the man off-balance, and the two crashed into the wall. "Run," he hissed at Sofia. As Nick forced Cal's arm up so the gun pointed at the ceiling, he stared into his sponsor's eyes.

Cal groaned, the knife still embedded deep in his calf. But the big man had a hundred pounds on Nick and he used his weight to drive Nick back. Wrenching his arm free, he tried to force the pistol against Nick's stomach, but Nick dropped his shoulder and drove into Cal's gut.

As the cop grabbed Nick's collar with his free hand, the gun went off, but the bullet embedded itself harmlessly into the far wall. Cal swung, and his fist connected with Nick's jaw, sending stars exploding behind his eyes. Nick sank to his knees, dizzy.

This time, the gunshot almost deafened him. Cal's mouth opened, a strained gasp escaping before a second shot rang out, and the cop crumpled to the floor, blood staining his lips and his eyes vacant.

Nick stared past Cal's body. At the end of the hall, leaning heavily on Sofia, Damian Forlano tucked his gun back into his holster, staggered back against the wall, and sank to the floor.

"Nick," Sofia said as she ran back to him.

He'd never heard a sweeter sound. His pain a distant memory, he got to his feet and caught her as she threw her arms around him.

Damian called weakly, "Somebody's going to have to carry me out of here. That *stronzo* shot me right after you ran out of the room, Nick."

Thundering footsteps echoed down the adjoining hall, and Damian hefted his gun with shaking hands.

"Boss? *Capo? Dove se?*"

"*Qui!*" Damian grunted.

Mario rounded the corner. "*Vaffanculo,*" he muttered when he saw Damian on the floor. In the next breath, he looked Nick and Sofia up and down. "*Merda.* If I get the boss, can you two walk? We got the girls safe outside and a couple of ambulances on the way." As he helped Damian up, he continued. "The cops loyal to your cousin Vito should be here soon, *capo.* We only had to kill two of the traffickers."

"All the girls?" Sofia asked, sinking against Nick. "Gina?"

Mario chuckled. "That's the one with the smart mouth and that tiny diamond in her nose? She's fine. Pissed off no one will let her back inside to look for you. Come on."

Leaning on one another, Nick and Sofia left Cal's body behind them and followed Mario into the cool, crisp evening air.

By the time they reached the group of ambulances, the blood loss left Nick cold and dizzy. But he'd walk another ten miles if he could keep Sofia at his side.

"Sof!" A young woman with the same hair, lips, and chin as his love ran towards them. Gina wrapped Sofia in a tight embrace, and Nick took a step back, then another, as the sisters sobbed in one another's arms.

When the EMTs came to lead the pair to one of the waiting ambulances, something inside Nick broke. He ached to follow, but the two of them had been through something horrible together, and he'd be in the way.

His hip burned. He scanned the area for an unoccupied ambulance or even Damian's car. Somewhere to lie down until the police needed him.

A cool hand touched his arm, and the scent of his love soothed his pain. "Don't leave"— tears stained Sofia's cheeks, and she sniffled —"me."

"Your sister..." He nodded to Gina, standing a few feet away with a weak smile curving her lips. "She needs you."

"And *I* need *you*." Sofia stepped closer, cupping his cheek, sliding her fingers through his hair. "I thought...the whole time I was terrified I'd never be able to tell you..." With a hiccup, she rested her cheek against his chest.

"I love you, Sofia." Nick couldn't hold his declaration back another moment. "When I left you—shite, was that only this morning?—I knew. You're it for me."

Sofia wrapped her arms around his neck. He didn't care that his leg shook from the effort of remaining upright or that almost two dozen people watched as she pressed her lips to his. Nick's tongue sought entrance, and she yielded, moaning into his kiss as his hands cupped her ass.

"Mr. Fairhaven?" A uniformed EMT interrupted them. "You're losing a fair amount of blood. We need to get you to the hospital. Ms. Oliviera, if you'll go with Mark over there—"

"I'm staying with Nick." She locked her arm with his. When the EMT protested, she glared at him. "Look at me," she squinted at his name tag, "Jason. Do I look like someone you want to argue with right now?"

"She's not," Gina piped up from behind Sofia. "Sofia saved all of us. You do *not* want to fuck with an Oliviera. Trust me."

Jason led Nick—with Sofia at his side and Gina trailing behind—over to a waiting ambulance. As he collapsed onto the gurney, Sofia leaned down and touched her forehead to his. "I love you, too."

## 26

Nick

THE NURSE RUSHED off with the suture kit as Damian Forlano pushed through Nick's hospital room

"Ever hear of knocking?" Nick asked as he eased into a pair of scrub pants. Balling up his bloody shirt, he tossed the stained material into the trash.

"I thought you'd be happy to see me." The mobster sported a sling sank carefully onto the edge of the hospital bed. "Or don't you care about what happened once the police arrived?"

"Tell me." Though Nick ached to find Sofia, he'd been ordered to stay put until the entire bag of IV fluids had emptied.

Damian scratched at the strap of the sling. "Leo is in custody. Anton—the man who took young Gina—is dead. Your *friend* lived.

"Cal."

"*Si*. The New Jersey Human Trafficking Unit is questioning him now. He made a single, very stupid decision a few months ago, Nick. He started gambling again, and he did not come to me for money. He went to Leo. The Russian *stronzo* was one of his paid informants for a time."

Betrayal sliced through Nick's heart. "We went to meetings. At least twice a month. But..." Nick searched his memories. "The last time he shared his story was more than a year ago."

"And Victor?" The last of the fluids dripped into his IV. Groaning as the new stitches pulled, Nick slid the needle from his arm. "What did his poker game have to do with any of this?"

"Very little. Except to draw in powerful men Leo could black-mail. Cal got his start there. Four other members of the Boston Police Department were regular attendees, along with the mayor's chief of staff." Damian shook his head, wincing. "Victor was arrested an hour ago."

Nick carefully drew a muddy green scrubs shirt over his head. "And the charges against me?"

"Dropped. You are a free man, Nick." With a grunt, Damian rose and held out his hand. "If you ever want to do business again —legitimately—contact me. You are calm in a crisis and have more intelligence than I gave you credit for."

The two men shook, and Nick chuckled. "As do you. But I still hope I never see you again."

After some well-placed threats to the doctors who didn't want him checking himself out of the hospital, Nick knocked softly on the door to Sofia's room. They wanted to keep her for observation overnight. But tests had ruled out a concussion. When she waved him in, her eyes were tired, but clear.

"Where's Gina?" Nick asked as took her hand and brushed a kiss over the bandage around her wrist.

"Making the rounds to see the other girls. She was stuck in

that room for three days. I don't think she can stand to sit still right now." Sofia twined their fingers and pulled him closer. "Hold me."

"I won't hurt you?" Nick eyed the bruises swelling along her cheek, neck, and shoulder.

Her snort led to a wince, but then she offered him a shy smile. "You're the one who got shot."

"Anesthetic is a wonderful invention." Toeing off his shoes, he fitted himself against her in the small hospital bed. He'd tossed his bloodstained clothes, opting for the rough green scrubs a nurse had been kind enough to offer him. Skimming a knuckle along the only part of her cheek not swollen and purple, he asked, "How are you?"

"Scared. Angry. Unsure about everything."

The furrow returned to her brow, and Nick smoothed his thumb over the wrinkle. "Everything?" He wasn't proud of the rough edge to his voice.

Sofia's eyes softened, the gold flecks glowing brighter. "Not us." She fiddled with the thin, rough blanket. "I did everything right. Checked the peephole, asked...Cal...what he wanted. He said you ordered lunch for me. It sounded so much like something you'd do...I didn't have any reason not to believe him."

Nick stilled her restless fingers, letting the connection between them calm his racing thoughts. He wanted so desperately to believe there'd been some reason—beyond falling off the wagon—for Cal's cruelty. For hurting Sofia. For shooting him. For cocking the hammer in preparation to kill him.

"Cal knew I went to a meeting. No phones in there. I was unreachable. He had at least a two-hour window to take you where no one would know." Nick's voice cracked, and he pressed his lips to the top of Sofia's head. "He played me from the beginning. I should have seen it. I'm an addict, love. I missed all the signs of his relapse."

Sofia made a soft, contemplative sound as she snuggled

closer. "He was your friend. When he took me, he told me he was sorry. Everything's fuzzy...whatever he gave me...I've never had such a headache. But...I think he was telling the truth." She sighed, the rough fabric of her hospital gown rustling under the sheets. "He preyed on you when you were at your lowest, Nick. And in the end, you saved me. You saved us."

"No, you did that, love." Nick smoothed his hand over her hair, careful to avoid the large bump on the side of her head. "You got away. You called Damian. Without that phone number..." He couldn't let himself think about what might have happened to her. "I don't want to ever let you out of my sight again."

"You know that's not practical, right?" Her voice held the slightest hint of laughter over the undercurrent of sadness. "I start school in a month. I hope, anyway. You really don't want to go to class with me. There will be tests. And boring lectures. Papers."

"If you wanted me there, I'd be there." Nick eased back so he could look her in the eyes. "I meant what I said, Sofia. I love you. I've done this dance before. Once...even seriously. I've never felt for anyone what I feel for you. I want you living at my flat—or ours—I'll move if you want. Closer to your school. I don't want to sleep anywhere other than a bed we share. And..." He trailed a finger along her neck, careful to avoid the marks one of Leo's men had made on her skin. "Will you wear my collar?"

"I can't. As much as I want to...I can't." As his heart started to crumble, she captured his hand. "Not yet."

Hope flared, the flame burning brightly inside him.

Sofia met his gaze, and he found only love reflected back at him. "I have to take care of Gina for a little while. Make sure she's okay. See if she wants to try for a deferment on her internship, help her get counseling. Find a therapist for myself."

"You don't have to take care of me any longer, Sis." Gina cleared her throat from the doorway. Like Nick, she wore a pair of green hospital scrubs. She'd washed her hair, scrubbed her makeup from her face, and sported a wrist brace from her fight with Leo. She extended her uninjured hand to Nick. "I'm Gina. I don't think we've been properly introduced."

Nick climbed awkwardly to his feet, his hip protesting the movement, and captured her hand between both of his. "Nick. I wish we were meeting under better circumstances."

Gina cracked a wry smile. "Well, Sof and I escaped something few women ever do. No one's seriously hurt—except the bad guys —and the two of you are making googly eyes at one another like you're soul mates. You want happier? You've got high standards."

His deep laugh freed him from the last serious strain pressing down on his shoulders. "You're right. Perhaps my perspective is a bit skewed."

Gina reached out for Sofia's hand, the three of them united in their attempts to heal. "I'm not going to let a week of bad decisions screw up the best job I could have ever hoped for. I have to take this chance. If I don't, I'll regret it for the rest of my life. I'll cancel the backpacking trip. Spend that time...doing what I should have been doing for the past ten years."

"What's that?" Sofia asked.

Gina frowned, and the same little furrow appeared between her brows. "I spent a lot of time...not appreciating you...I have to make up for, Sis."

Sofia's pride in her sister shone through the bruises and the exhaustion. "Are you sure?"

"Yes. Until I leave, I want us to spend some serious time together. But...it's pretty obvious that the two of you love one another. Doing nothing but sitting in a tiny room waiting to be...*sold*...for two days gives you a lot of time to think. To regret. To vow to do things differently if given the chance. Sof, you put your life on hold for me for ten years. It's time you came first. If you want to move in with Nick, do it. Life is too short to wait."

"Sofia, what *do* you want?" Nick asked, easing his uninjured hip onto the bed.

She looked from Gina to Nick, her fingers fluttering over the edge of the blanket again. "I don't want to go back to our apartment. I want to...to maybe get my own place for a while, but also..." She smiled, and Nick's world righted. "Ask me again. Once I'm settled somewhere for a little bit—hopefully not too far from you—ask me again."

His heart tightened in his chest, hope and love warring for dominance. Nick gently framed her face, being careful of her myriad of bruises. "I'll ask you again. And again and again and again until you say yes or tell me to stop. There's nothing I wouldn't do to make you happy."

Sofia's eyelids fluttered, and she sighed, exhaustion straining her features. "Hold me tonight. That's all I want right now."

With a quick peck to her sister's forehead, Gina straightened. "I'm going to check on Emily. I'll probably sleep in her room tonight. She's feeling pretty crappy after a week with so little food and her parents won't get here until tomorrow. I'm right next door." Before she turned to go, she wrapped her arms around Nick and gave him a gentle squeeze. "Take care of my big sister."

He met Gina's gaze, more serious than he'd ever been. "Always."

**Sofia**

At the security checkpoint, Sofia hugged her sister and tried not to cry. "I'm going to miss you," she whispered in Gina's ear. "Be careful."

"You'll talk to me all the time. We live in the age of FaceTime, remember? And my HR contact set me up in a secured building, the internet's already turned on, and there's even a car service to take me to and from work for the first month." Gina smiled, but her eyes glistened with unshed tears. "I'm as safe as I can be."

"And you'll find a therapist?" Sofia grasped Gina's fingers, longing for one last moment of connection before her sister flew away to start her new life.

With what could only be called a self-satisfied smile, Gina chuckled. "Already done. The trauma counselor at Mass General hooked me up. You don't have to take care of me anymore, Sof."

"I'll always take care of you, baby girl." After one last fierce embrace, Sofia let her sister go.

Nick slid his arm around Sofia's waist and let her lean against him as Gina blended into the security line. In the past ten days, he'd moved both of them into a vacant condo in his building, "borrowed" several of his brother's staff to set up the place, had given them a key to his unit, and, most importantly, had let Sofia set the tone and pace of what happened next.

Though she'd intended to take some time alone, most nights, she'd invited him into her bed, and he'd been all too happy to oblige. Last night, though, the two sisters shared a bottle of wine, sappy movies, and stories of their parents until three in the morning. Alone.

"Take me home?" Sofia turned in his arms and peered up at him, her hands splayed over his chest. "We haven't...played since...before."

Despite his obvious arousal every time he shared her bed, Nick had yet to make love to her, and she'd been too unsure, too focused on figuring out her own emotions to ask for what she now desperately needed—to feel normal.

"Are you sure, kitten?" His voice took on a hint of authority. She shifted her hips against him, and her nipples peaked under her sweater. Not his full Master persona, but close enough. "I haven't wanted to...trigger any painful memories." He ran his fingers over the scars on her wrists. "Or hurt you."

"There are a lot of things you can do without tying me up,"

she teased. "And...even that...your ropes don't frighten me. They're...love. I'm ready to try. You've given me space, and I needed it. But I've missed you."

"My dear Sofia, I was never more than a staircase away. Nor will I ever be."

"Until next week. Then you'll be at work, and I'll be at school, and I'll only get to see you in the evenings." Nick's active role in the rescue of seven women hours before they were to be sold had gone a long way with the press—and the Board of Fairhaven Exports. While Alex would continue to run the company and serve as CEO, Nick had accepted a position of Chief Operations Officer and would return to work in a few days. When he'd shared the news with her, he'd looked a bit like a kid on Christmas.

Sofia slid her hand up to cup the back of his neck. "When does the sublease run out?"

"Any time you want. There's been no interest in the unit. The condo board is letting me rent it month-to-month." Hope colored his tone, and he broke into a wide smile. "Does this mean...?"

"I worried I'd only be moving in because I was scared." Sofia shook her head. "That's a horrible thing to do to a relationship. But I've been talking to my therapist about it. Life is too short, and I love you. I'm ready."

Nick dipped his head and sealed his lips over hers. As his kiss warmed her down to her toes, Sofia knew she'd found her home.

**Nick**

He hadn't been this nervous since the day he first walked in the door of Fairhaven Tower. Returning to work—after all that had happened—both thrilled and terrified him. Dipping his hand into his pocket, he fingered the eighteen-month chip.

Two days ago, Detective Sampson had knocked on his door. Sofia had answered, and when she'd rushed into the bedroom, fear churning in her eyes, he'd been prepared for the worst. But the detective had merely stopped by to return the well-worn coin.

*"This was found in Emily Norse's apartment. When we interviewed her after the rescue, she told us Calloway Pritchard drugged her, then as she lay on the floor, unable to move, he kicked something small and metallic under her coffee table."*

Hearing about yet another betrayal had reopened the wounds in Nick's heart that might never fully heal, but he felt better with his talisman back in his pocket. The previous night at his regular meeting, he'd told his story—a slightly sanitized version that didn't include Damian Forlano's involvement.

Now, he rapped on his brother's open office door.

"Nicholas. Have a seat," Alex said with a hint of a smile. The bags had almost disappeared from under his eyes, but a deep sadness still lingered in the emerald depths.

Sitting carefully, his hip still tender, he leaned forward. "How's Elizabeth?"

"Better." Running a hand through his hair, Alex sighed. "We'd just decided to try, you know. Not more than three months ago. Neither of us expected we'd succeed so quickly. When her father died, I didn't want her to go to Seattle. I knew something was wrong. I *felt* it."

"You couldn't have prevented this, Alex." Nick fixed his brother with a firm stare. "Even if you'd tried...kept her home, the stress of losing her father..."

"I know." Alex twisted his wedding ring on his finger. The diamonds winked in the office lights. "She's my entire world, Nicholas. She has been since the moment I first spoke to her. For a few weeks, my world expanded with our child. Now, there's a gaping hole where he or she would have been. "

Nick pushed to his feet, skirted the corner of Alex's desk, and rested his hand on his brother's shoulder. "Anything you need, you know you just have to ask."

When Alex looked up at him, the weeks of frustration, the tense messages, the fights over Nick's supposed behavior all fell away, and his younger brother sought his approval and comfort. "Come to dinner tomorrow. We'd love to meet Sofia. Elizabeth and I...we need our family right now."

Nodding, emotion welling in his throat, Nick squeezed his brother's shoulder. "We'll be there."

"Well, then." Alex stood, enveloping Nick in a quick, fierce hug. "Shall we go to the board meeting? You can recount your heroic efforts. Perhaps that will be enough to remind a few of the more cantankerous tossers just whose name is on the building."

"Let's go have a little fun," Nick said, matching his brother's smile. "After you."

# EPILOGUE

**Two months later**

**Nick**

HIS GAZE KEPT WANDERING to the dresser as he waited for Sofia to finish getting dressed. His brother and Elizabeth would be here in a few minutes, and he didn't know if he could wait until the end of the evening when they would be alone again.

"I'm sorry," she said breathlessly as she tugged the peach blouse over her head. "If Professor Marx hadn't been two hours late for the review session, I would have been home in plenty of time."

"Don't fret." Nick brushed an errant curl away from her face. "You look lovely."

Sofia ducked out of his reach to detour to the dresser. A quick spritz of perfume from the delicate glass bottle infused the room, and Nick inhaled deeply, waiting for the moment she'd notice the black, velvet box.

Too distracted, however, she rushed into to the walk-in closet.

"How do you own more shoes than I do?" She emerged dangling a pair of strappy black sandals from her fingers. "And how do you always look so...put together?"

"Boarding school." He tucked the box under his arm as she dropped onto the settee at the foot of the bed. "The headmaster would give us demerits if our shirts weren't starched, or if a single crease was out of place. The day I spilled gravy on my tie is one I'll never forget."

She laughed, one of his favorite sounds in the world. A brief mental image of her bent over the padded bench, her arms spread wide and bound to the bedposts, her thighs reddened from his flogger stirred his cock, and he cursed the time as he glanced at his watch.

"What?" Sofia tipped her gaze to his, concern forming the small crease between her brows he loved so much. "You're standing there like you're about to tell me the world is ending."

*It might...if I screw this up.*

Nick sank down next to her, sliding the box behind him and then taking her hands. "Are you happy?"

The furrow deepened. "Yes. Completely." When he couldn't immediately continue, Sofia filled the silence. "We didn't do this the—normal?—way. Three weeks from meeting to living together? With...what happened...in between? Most people would think we were crazy."

During her therapy, their occasional nightmares, and the friends-and-family GA meetings she'd attended with him, Sofia had rarely used the words kidnapping or sex trafficking. But alone with him, in the semi-darkness lit by the single night light that burned twenty-four-seven, they'd healed together, sometimes talking until sunrise.

She squeezed his fingers. "I believe in fate, Nick. So did my mother. Sometimes, you have to take a chance. To leap without more than a quick look at what's beneath you."

Letting out the breath he hadn't known he was holding, Nick

slipped a hand free. When he set the box on her knees, her mouth formed a little *o,* her lower lip wobbling slightly.

*Shite. She's going to say no.*

He couldn't turn back now. *I'll ask you again. And again and again and again until you say yes or tell me to stop. There's nothing I wouldn't do to make you happy.* The promise he'd made her in the hospital drove him forward.

"I love you, Sofia. I may have fallen in love with you the first night we met." Fumbling for the catch on the box, he lifted the lid.

"Ohhh."

A simple gold chain with eight small, equally spaced diamonds rested on an angled bed of velvet. Every piece of jewelry Sofia owned was simple. Understated. He'd resisted the urge to buy her the most expensive collar he could afford. Instead, he'd called Gina, and the two of them had looked at designs for a week before he'd settled on this one.

In place of the clasp, the collar had a small lock that required a unique pin to open.

"I know you want to finish school before any talk of marriage. Though, in truth, I'd marry you tomorrow if you changed your mind. But...for now..."

Nick lifted the collar from the box and dropped to one knee. "Sofia, will you wear my collar? Will you commit yourself to me? As my submissive. But also as my partner."

Golden flecks danced in the dark brown of her eyes. "Yes," she whispered. "Yes, I'll wear your collar. Yes to all of it. Sir."

He rose, led her over to the mirror, and stepped behind her to fasten the chain around her neck.

Sofia ran her fingers over the gold. "It's beautiful."

"It's you." Nick brushed the first diamond. "For your smile, that warms me in places that haven't seen the sun in years." Trailing his finger down to the second jewel, he continued. "For your strength, because without you, I'd still be lost. For your tears that I'll kiss away, every day for the rest of our lives—"

Sofia turned in his arms and claimed his mouth. He backed her up against the dresser, cupping her breast and dragging his thumb over her nipple. She moaned, and when he pulled away, his cock strained against his briefs. Only the doorbell stopped him from ripping her clothes off and taking her.

"We will continue this later, kitten," he said, his tone taking on the strong, confident edge he knew she loved.

"Yes, Sir." As she rushed out of the bedroom to answer the door, he thought her heard her say, "I'm counting on it."

Despite the new-found closeness he and Alex now shared, this was one night Nick couldn't wait for his brother to go home. He and Elizabeth had healed as well as anyone could from the loss they experienced and Elizabeth's doctor had given them the okay to try again—as long as Elizabeth avoided as much stress as possible.

Exchanging hugs all around, the four confirmed their plans for the following week—dinner at Strega—and then Nick and Sofia were finally alone.

"Strip down to your panties and bra," he ordered as he flicked open the top button of his shirt. "Kneel on the bed, spread your legs, and clasp your hands behind you."

"Yes, Sir." Sofia tugged her blouse over her head before she reached the hallway, and once Nick had checked the locks and set the security system, he unbuttoned his shirt as he strode into the bedroom.

*Fuck me.*

She was a vision. Pale, peach lace stood out dramatically

against her dusky skin. The diamonds around her neck sparkled in the spotlights over the bed, and with her hands clasped at the small of her back, her breasts thrust forward, the stiff peaks begging for his teeth.

"Are you green, kitten?"

Raising her eyes, Sofia smiled. "Yes, Sir. Very, very green."

Nick withdrew padded cuffs from the nightstand and dangled them in front of her. "You enjoyed these last week. Will you try them again? I don't have to bind you."

Sofia held out her wrists. The scars had faded, though Nick would never forget the extent of her wounds. "Bind me, Sir. Control my pleasure. I trust you completely."

When he had her naked and spread-eagled on *their* bed, a thought that brought him joy every single day, he worshipped her body. Dragging a thumb over her nipple, kissing down her stomach, briefly sweeping his tongue through her slick folds. She could move her head and her hips, but not much else, and she pulled at her restraints when he lavished attention on her clit.

"Please, Sir. I need more."

"More?" he asked from between her legs. "What more could you want from your Master?"

"You...bought something new...last week," she said between shudders and low, keening cries. "You...promised you'd use them...on me, Sir." Her hips ground into the mattress, trying for the smallest bit of relief, but she'd find none. Not until he was ready to release her from this sweet torture.

With a chuckle, Nick leaned over and yanked on the nightstand drawer. His Sofia enjoyed a bit of pain. Palming her breast, he pinched and sucked on her nipple until he knew it had to be throbbing, then attached the clamp. Sofia cried out, her back arching. "Yes! Please, Sir. The other one."

"As you wish."

When the second clip went on, she thrashed her head about. "I can't hold on much longer."

He dove back between her legs, relishing in the sweet taste of her arousal. Her thighs quivered, then her stomach, and a quick glance at her restrained hands showed him she'd balled her fingers, trying desperately to hold back her release until he'd given her permission.

With a rustle of foil, he withdrew the condom, and once he'd sheathed himself, he grabbed her hips and slid home. One thrust, two, three, and he wanted this night to go on forever. But his sweet sub couldn't hold on much longer, and there were many more hours until dawn.

"Come for me, kitten. Open your eyes and let me see you fly." Bracing himself, he held her gaze as he rammed his hips into her again, and again, until she screamed his name. With a final thrust, he followed her over the edge, soaring alongside her through a release made so much sweeter by their new commitment to one another.

A few minutes later, when he'd drawn a blanket over them, but not released her from the cuffs, he skimmed his finger over the diamonds at her throat. "You know, you didn't let me finish earlier. Explaining why I'd picked each diamond."

"Don't tell me, Sir," Sofia said with a challenge in her gaze. "Show me."

* * *

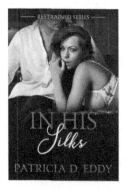

NICK AND SOFIA almost lost everything. I don't know about you, but I was a little nervous there for a while. If this is the first book in the Restrained Series you've read, perhaps you'd like to pick up **IN HIS SILKS**.

*One touch, and he was lost.*

He's the richest man in Boston. With a

single look, he can have any woman he wants.

Except her. Elizabeth won't give him the time of day—except to tell him she's so far out of his social circle, she might as well be from another planet.

In Elizabeth's eyes, Alexander sees not only a lifetime of pain but an untrained submissive unlike any he's ever met—one with fire and strength and fierce intelligence. He aches to show her the joys of submission.

Happiness doesn't come easily, though. Especially not when a billion dollar tax fraud case threatens Alexander's company—and Elizabeth's life.

The scars from Elizabeth's past run deep, and if she can't give Alexander her trust, she could lose so much more than a chance at love.

Danger lurks in the unlikeliest of places, and more than one life is at stake.

He'll risk everything for the woman he loves, but Elizabeth is fiercely independent. Will she accept his protection—and his domination? Or will he lose her forever?

**_One-click TODAY to find out!_**

IF YOU LOVED In His Collar, you'll love **BREAKING HIS CODE**, my sensual, geeky, and thrilling military romance.

*"It was easier to run away than watch another guy decide I'm too much trouble—too broken or too slow or too...me."*

—

Camilla Delgado. Computer genius. Former explosives ordinance expert. Wounded on the dusty roads of

Afghanistan, she exchanged her dreams of adventure for a life behind a computer. Trapped by her cane—and her scars—Cam avoids the "real" world whenever she can.

Until her newest online gaming buddy asks her out for coffee.

West, a former Navy SEAL, looks more like a cover model for Men's Health than a human being. And his slight drawl? Hotter than the espresso Cam spills down her shirt.

But Cam doesn't **do** charming. And all of her instincts scream, "RUN!"

West doesn't understand what he said—or did—to drive his sexy and smart gaming partner away. She set him ablaze, and nothing can put out these flames.

Unable to forget the man who saw *her* and not her scars, Cam lets West draw her out of her shell.

Now, she's hot on the trail of a hacker threatening her career while navigating the minefield of falling in love.

When ghosts from West's past and fears for the future threaten, will Cam find the courage to lower her defenses and let him in?

—

_BREAKING HIS CODE_ is a standalone romantic suspense featuring the men and women of Emerald City Security and Hidden Agenda K&R. Meet these former military heroes and computer geniuses who'll show you just how steamy and heart-wrenching love can be.

Can broken be beautiful?

*Hell, yes.*

One-click **BREAKING HIS CODE** now!

* * *

You can also join my Facebook group, **Patricia's Unstoppable Forces**, for exclusive giveaways, sneak peeks of future books, and the chance to see your name in a future novel!

**P.S. Reviews are like candy for authors.**

Did you know that reviews are like chocolate (or cookies or cake) for authors?

They're also the most powerful tool I have to sell more books. I can't take out full page ads in the newspaper or put ads on the side of buses.

Not yet, anyway.

But I have something more powerful and effective than ads.

**A loyal (and smart) bunch of readers.**

Honest reviews of my books help bring them to the attention of other readers.

If you've enjoyed this book, I'd be eternally grateful if you could spend just five minutes leaving a review (it can be as short as you like) on the book's Amazon page.

# ALSO BY PATRICIA D. EDDY

## By the Fates

Check out the By the Fates series if you love dark and steamy tales of witches, devils, and an epic battle between good and evil.

By the Fates, Freed

Destined, a By the Fates Story

By the Fates, Fought

By the Fates, Fulfilled

\* \* \*

## In Blood

If you love hot Italian vampires and and a human who can hold her own against beings far stronger, then the In Blood series is for you.

Secrets in Blood

Revelations in Blood

\* \* \*

## Contemporary and Erotic Romances

\* \* \*

## Holidays and Heroes

Beauty isn't only skin deep and not all scars heal. Come swoon over sexy vets and the men and women who love them.

Mistletoe and Mochas

Love and Libations

\* \* \*

## Away From Keyboard

Dive into a steamy mix of geekery and military might with the men and women of Emerald City Security and Hidden Agenda Services.

Breaking His Code

In Her Sights

On His Six

\* \* \*

## Restrained

Do you like to be tied up? Or read about characters who do? Enjoy a fresh BDSM series that will leave you begging for more.

In His Silks

Christmas Silks

All Tied Up For New Year's

In His Collar

# ABOUT THE AUTHOR

I've always made up stories. Sometimes I even acted them out. I probably shouldn't admit that my childhood best friend and I used to run around the backyard pretending to fly in our Invisible Jet and rescue Steve Trevor. Oops.

Now that I'm too old to spin around in circles with felt magic bracelets on my wrists, I put "pen to paper" instead. Figuratively, at least. Fingers to keyboard is more accurate.

Outside of my writing, I'm a professional editor, a software geek, a singer (in the shower only), and a runner. I love red wine, scotch (neat, please), and cider. Seattle is my home, and I share an old house with my husband and cats.

I'm on my fourth—fifth?—rewatching of the modern *Doctor Who*, and I think one particular quote from that show sums up my entire life.

"We're all stories, in the end. Make it a good one, eh?" — *The Eleventh Doctor, Doctor Who*

I hope your story is brilliant.

*You can reach me all over the web...*
patriciadeddy.com
patricia@patriciadeddy.com

Made in the USA
Coppell, TX
19 March 2023